HARLEQUIN®
Presents

Summer's here, and to get you in the mood we've got some sizzling reads for you this month!

So relax and enjoy…a scandalous proposal in *Bought for Revenge, Bedded for Pleasure* by Emma Darcy; a virgin bride in *Virgin: Wedded at the Italian's Convenience* by Diana Hamilton; a billionaire's bargain in *The Billionaire's Blackmailed Bride* by Jacqueline Baird; a sexy Spaniard in *Spanish Billionaire, Innocent Wife* by Kate Walker; and an Italian's marriage ultimatum in *The Salvatore Marriage Deal* by Natalie Rivers. And be sure to read *The Greek Tycoon's Baby Bargain*, the first book in Sharon Kendrick's brilliant new duet, GREEK BILLIONAIRES' BRIDES.

Plus, two new authors bring you their dazzling debuts—Natalie Anderson with *His Mistress by Arrangement*, and Anne Oliver with *Marriage at the Millionaire's Command*. Don't miss out!

We'd love to hear what you think about Presents. E-mail us at Presents@hmb.co.uk or join in the discussions at www.iheartpresents.com and www.sensationalromance.blogspot.com, where you'll also find more information about books and authors!

RED HOT REVENGE

There are times in a man's life...

when only seduction will settle old scores!

Pick up our exciting series of revenge-filled
romances—they're recommended and red-hot!

Available only from Harlequin Presents®

Jacqueline Baird

THE BILLIONAIRE'S BLACKMAILED BRIDE

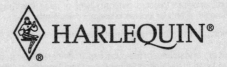

RED HOT REVENGE

◆ HARLEQUIN®

TORONTO • NEW YORK • LONDON
AMSTERDAM • PARIS • SYDNEY • HAMBURG
STOCKHOLM • ATHENS • TOKYO • MILAN • MADRID
PRAGUE • WARSAW • BUDAPEST • AUCKLAND

ISBN-13: 978-0-373-12733-7
ISBN-10:   0-373-12733-2

THE BILLIONAIRE'S BLACKMAILED BRIDE

First North American Publication 2008.

All about the author...
Jacqueline Baird

JACQUELINE BAIRD was born and raised in Northumbria, U.K. She met her husband when she was eighteen. Eight years later, after many adventures around the world, she came home and married him. They still live in Northumbria, and have two grown-up sons.

Jacqueline's number-one passion is writing. She has always been an avid reader and she had her first success as a writer at the age of eleven, when she won first prize in the Nature Diary of the Year competition at school. But she always felt a little guilty because her diary was more fiction than fact.

She always loved romance novels and when her sons went to school all day, she thought she would try writing one. She's been writing for the Harlequin Presents line ever since, and she still gets a thrill every time a new book is published.

When Jacqueline is not busy writing, she likes to spend her time traveling, reading and playing cards. She was a keen sailor until a knee injury ended her sailing days, but she still enjoys swimming in the sea when the weather allows.

She visits a gym three times a week and has made the surprising discovery that she gets some good ideas while doing the mind-numbingly boring exercises on the cycling and weight machines.

CHAPTER ONE

'I STILL can't believe you chose this for me,' Emily Fairfax said with a shake of her head as she sat down opposite her older brother Tom and his wife Helen at their table in the vast ballroom of the deluxe London hotel. 'I feel terribly conspicuous.' Embarrassment coloured her face almost as red as the outfit she was wearing.

'Oh, lighten up, Emily. You look great.' Tom grinned at her. 'This is a costume ball for Dad's favourite charity, The Children of Africa's Guardian Angel Project; he would have appreciated the Devil and Angels theme. Dad had a great sense of humour. Remember Mum's fortieth when he insisted everyone dress as Knights and Squires? I think he would have seen the funny side…'

'All too well. Most of the women ended up looking like young boys, dressed in doublet and hose. I wondered at the time if Dad had secret gay tendencies,' she quipped and then turned her sparkling blue gaze on her sister-in-law, a petite gamine-faced brunette. 'But this is different, Helen. There is nothing funny about being squeezed into a red latex suit that is a couple of sizes too small. What on earth were you thinking of when you ordered it?' she demanded, and saw the mischief dancing in Helen's brown eyes and her lips twisted in a wry smile.

Tom and Helen had met at university and had married two

years ago at the age of twenty-three. They were now the proud parents of a one-year-old daughter, who had been born the week before Tom and Emily's father had died suddenly of a massive heart attack. The child was named Sara after their mother, who had died three years earlier after a long battle with cancer.

'I don't know what you are complaining about. You look fine, and I went to a lot of trouble to get that costume in the right size. At four and a half months pregnant I am actually the same bust measurement as you and I tried it on to make sure it would fit,' Helen said with a grin.

'Did it never occur to you that you're five feet nothing and I am five nine—that it would have to go a little further on me?' Emily groaned. 'You damn near broke my neck pulling the hood over my head. It is still aching.' She slipped a hand beneath the heavy fall of her hair and rubbed the nape of her neck to emphasize the point.

'Don't blame me. If you had come back to London yesterday as you were supposed to, you would have had time to get your own costume. But instead you spent another day on site and only arrived a couple of hours before the event. Plus it is April Fool's Day,' she said with an impish grin. 'And be fair—I did cut the hood off and twist it into a braid so you could wear the horns as a head band.' She burst out laughing.

Emily bit her lip to fight down the answering grin that threatened. She had totally forgotten it was the first of April, and Helen was right—she should have returned from Santorini yesterday instead of flying into London this evening. She really had no one to blame but herself, but she wasn't going to let her beloved sister-in-law off too easy.

'Anyone with a grain of common sense would have ordered an angel costume for me. The same as yours, I might add. It is only logical that the women dress as angels and the men as devils. Like my idiot brother T—'

'Excuse me.' A deep, slightly accented voice cut into Emily's good-natured tirade. 'Hello, Tom, nice to see you again.'

'Anton, glad you and your friends could make it.'

Emily looked over at her brother as he greeted the new arrivals he had invited to make up their table of eight.

She glanced up at the man who had so rudely interrupted her. His back was turned to her and he was pulling out a chair for his companion, a stunning brunette who naturally was dressed like an angel in a diaphanous gold and white fabric that seemed to reveal a lot more flesh than Emily imagined any self-respecting angel would reveal.

At least her outfit covered her from neck to toe, she consoled herself, though she had been forced to undo the front zip a few inches to prevent the damn thing crushing her chest so tightly she could barely breathe. It wasn't her usual style, that was for sure, but it didn't really faze her. She knew she had a decent enough body, she just wasn't used to displaying it quite so dramatically.

'Allow me to introduce my friend Eloise,' the deep voice continued as the brunette sent a social smile around the table, 'and my right-hand man, Max.'

Emily glanced at the middle-aged burly man and smiled in welcome as he took his seat at the table next to Helen. Then the stranger turned to her.

'Emily, isn't it? Tom has told me a lot about you. It is a real pleasure to finally meet you. I am Anton Diaz.' A large strong hand was held out and she politely put her hand in his, while her mind busily wondered how Tom knew the man, and why her brother would have mentioned her to him.

Then suddenly her mind went blank as a bizarre sensation a bit like an electric eel snaking up her arm had her skin breaking out in goose-bumps under the latex. Hastily she pulled her hand free and slowly looked up.

Emily had a long way to go… He had to be at least six feet four, she reckoned, and then her curious blue gaze collided with deep brown eyes and she simply stared…

The man was like a sleek black panther: poised, powerful and predatory.

She grimaced inwardly at the fanciful notion, really not her usual style.

The introductions moved on and Emily supposed she had made the right response, though she could not be sure. Her mouth felt dry and she had trouble tearing her fascinated gaze away from the tall, striking man.

He was dressed all in black. A black silk-knit roll-necked sweater outlined the impressive musculature of his broad chest. A short black cloak covered his wide shoulders and flowed down like bats' wings to broad cuffs around strong wrists, set off by tailored black trousers. He should have looked ridiculous in costume like the majority of the people present. Instead, if ever a man looked like a devil it was this one…

Dark and dangerous, she thought, her heart inexplicably tightening in her chest, and for a moment she had difficulty breathing that had nothing to do with the latex suit she wore.

His straight black hair worn slightly longer than was fashionable was swept casually back off his broad forehead. Distinctive arched brows framed deep-set almost black eyes, high cheekbones, a large hawklike nose and a wide sensuous mouth completed the picture. As she stared his lips parted to reveal even white teeth. He was smiling down at her. She lifted her eyes to his and even in her stunned state she recognized the humour did not entirely mask the cool remoteness of his dark gaze.

The man was not conventionally handsome, his features too large and harshly chiselled for classic male beauty.

Brutally handsome…was a better description.

There was something insulting about the way his dark eyes slid casually down to her cleavage and lingered for a long moment. But even as she recognized his insolent masculine appraisal for what it was her skin prickled with shocking awareness. The breath caught in her throat and she gave a shaky inward sigh of relief when he casually pulled out the chair next to hers, and lowered his long length into it.

It could be worse, Emily told herself, at least with Anton Diaz seated at her side, she did not have to face him.

Instinctively she recognized he was a man who was supremely confident in his masculinity and totally aware of his effect on the opposite sex, and discreetly she crossed her arms over her suddenly hardening nipples. A sophisticated charmer with an aura of ruthless power about him that would intimidate anybody, man or woman, she concluded. Not her type at all…

Even so, there was no escaping the fact he was an incredibly sexy man, as her body's unexpected response confirmed.

'I could not help overhearing your comment, Emily. Shame on you, your chauvinism is showing.' The devil spoke in a deep, dark, mocking voice that made her hackles rise.

'What do you mean, Mr Diaz?' she asked him with cool politeness, flicking him a sidelong glance, and was once again captured by the intensity of his dark eyes.

'In today's world of equality between the sexes isn't it rather politically incorrect to assume all the women should dress as angels and the men as devils? And, given the very striking outfit you are wearing, just a little hypocritical,' he drawled mockingly.

'He has got you there,' Helen piped up and everyone laughed. Everyone but Emily.

'My costume was my sister-in-law's choice, not mine. She has a warped sense of humour,' she explained, forcing a smile to her lips. 'And I see you are dressed as a devil, rather upholding my theory. Though you do seem to have forgotten the horns,' she prompted smoothly.

'No, I didn't forget. I never forget anything,' he asserted, his dark eyes holding hers with an intimacy that made her pulse race and she could do nothing about the pink that tinged her cheeks. 'I am supposed to be an angel, admittedly a dark angel, but an angel nevertheless.'

Emily saw what he meant, her blue eyes sweeping over him. It was the perfect costume for him. Unrelenting black and somehow threatening… She glimpsed a darkening in his deepset eyes and something more. Anger… Why? She had no idea, and in an attempt to control her overheated imagination and body she looked somewhere past his left shoulder. She took a deep steadying breath, but for a long moment was incapable of making a response. No man had ever had such a startling effect on her in her life, and she had met plenty, and been attracted to a few, but never quite like this.

She was a twenty-four-year-old freelance marine archaeologist and had spent the last two years since qualifying gaining experience in her field. She had been on a few seagoing explorations. Her colleagues were mostly men, explorers, divers and fellow archaeologists with the skills needed to search and map out underwater wrecks and artifacts. Yet never once had she felt the sudden heat, the stomach-churning excitement that this man aroused in her with one look.

Get a grip, girl, she told herself. He was with his very beautiful girlfriend and, while Emily considered herself passably attractive, she was no competition for the lovely Eloise.

What was she thinking of?

At twenty-one, after a disastrous engagement that had ended abruptly after three days when she had found her fiancé in bed with her flatmate at university, she had sworn off men.

Nigel had been an accountant in her father's firm. A man she had fallen in love with at sixteen, a man who had kissed her at her eighteenth birthday party and declared he felt the same, a man who had offered her comfort and support when her mother was ill and died, a man whose proposal she had accepted shortly after. A man who, when she had confronted him in bed with her flatmate, had actually admitted the affair had been going on for a year. Her flatmate, her supposed friend, twisted the knife by telling her she was a fool. Nigel's interest in Emily had only ever been for her money and connections.

Which was a laugh. Admittedly the family home was probably worth millions in today's market, but they lived in it, had done for generations. The business earned the shareholders a decent dividend each year but not a fortune by any means, but at the time she had felt utterly betrayed. She would no more compete for a man than fly to the moon, and, to be honest, over the intervening years, she had never felt the need. Which was probably why she had never since had a long-term relationship? she thought wryly.

'Yes, of course, I see it now, a silly mistake on my part,' she finally responded.

'You're forgiven,' he said with a smile that took her breath away all over again.

But at that moment the last two guests making up the table arrived and Emily smiled with relief. It was her aunt Lisa, her father's older sister, and her husband, James Browning, who was also the Chairman of the Board of Fairfax Engineering since her dad's death. She felt the light brush of Anton's shoulder against hers as, like a perfect gentleman, he stood up until Lisa was seated, and she determinedly ignored it.

Her equilibrium thankfully restored…

James took the seat on the other side of Emily. 'Aunt Lisa, Uncle James, it's good to see you,' she offered, her wayward emotions firmly under control.

But it was the *sotto voce* comment that Anton Diaz made among the flurry of introduction as he sat back down that threw her off balance yet again. 'But if a devil is more to your liking I'm sure something can be arranged.'

Her mouth open, her face scarlet, she stared at Anton. One dark brow rose in sardonic query, before he turned to respond to Eloise's rather loud request for champagne.

Was she hearing things? Had he actually made such a blatantly flirtatious comment or had she imagined what he said?

She did not know…and she did not know whether to feel angry or flattered as dinner was served. Emily's emotions stayed in pretty much the same state of flux until it was over; she was intensely aware of the man at her side.

The conversation was sociable, and when the meal ended and the band began to play Emily could not help watching Anton and Eloise as they took to the dance floor. Both Latin in looks, they made a striking couple and the way Eloise curved into her partner's body, her arms firmly clasped around his neck, left no one in any doubt of the intimacy of their relationship.

Emily turned to James and asked what she had been dying to ask all evening. Who exactly was Anton Diaz?

According to her uncle, Anton Diaz was the founder of a private equity business that made massive profits out of buying, restructuring and then selling on great chunks of worldwide businesses. It made him a man of enormous influence and power. It had also made him extremely rich. He was revered worldwide as a financial genius, with a fortune to match. His nationality was hazy, his name was hispanic, yet some considered him Greek because he spoke the language like a native. Rumours about him abounded. Her aunt Lisa offered the most colourful speculation that his grandmother had been the madam of a high-class brothel in Peru, and her daughter had been a wealthy Greek's mistress for years and Anton Diaz was the result of the affair.

Her aunt also informed her archly that he owned a magnificent villa on a Greek island, a vast estate in Peru, a luxurious apartment in New York and another in Sydney. Recently he had acquired a prestigious office block in London with a stunning penthouse at the top, and there were probably more. Plus the parties he held on his huge luxury yacht were legendary.

James attempted to steer the conversation back to less gossipy ground by continuing that he knew Anton was multilingual because he had heard him employ at least four languages when they had first met at a European conference a couple of months ago. Since then they had become business acquaintances and friends of a sort, hence Tom inviting Anton and his party to join them tonight. In fact, Anton Diaz's expert advice had been instrumental in them deciding to diversify and expand Fairfax Engineering, James informed her in an almost reverential tone.

It was news to Emily that the firm needed revising or expanding, but she had no time to dwell on that revelation as her aunt chimed in again. Apparently Anton was a confirmed bachelor and as famous for the women he had bedded as he was for his financial skills. His countless affairs were apparently well documented by the press, actresses and models featuring prominently.

Emily believed her uncle and aunt and in a sense felt relieved. Her earlier reaction to Anton Diaz had been normal under the circumstances. The man exuded a raw animal magnetism that probably affected every woman he met the same way, and if his press was to be believed he took full advantage of the fact. He was not the type of man any self-respecting woman would want to get involved with.

After her one disastrous relationship Emily had very firm ideas on the type of man she eventually wanted to marry. She wanted a like-minded man she could trust. Certainly not a womanizing, globe-trotting billionaire, plus she was in no hurry to marry—she enjoyed her work far too much to think of curtailing her career for any man for years yet.

Draining her coffee-cup, she smiled at James and Lisa affectionately as they decided to dance. Then looking around the table, she saw only the burly Max was left.

Emily was naturally a happy, confident girl with a successful career and a growing name in her field of expertise. She was also a realist and never let anything she could not change bother her for long. She was a firm believer in making the best of any situation. Neither the blatantly sexy costume she wore nor her strange reaction to the indomitable Anton Diaz was going to prevent her enjoying the evening.

'So, Max, would you like to dance?' she asked with a broad smile. She watched him blink, then grin and leap to his feet with alacrity.

'It will be my pleasure,' he said as he pulled out her chair. His brown eyes widened as she rose to her feet, sweeping over the length of her body with unconcealed admiration. 'You are a very lovely lady, señorita,' he said, taking her hand and leading her to the dance floor.

Max was about an inch taller than Emily, and quite a lot wider, but for a heavy man he was a very good dancer and surprisingly light on his feet. Emily relaxed in his hold and began to have fun.

* * *

Anton Diaz allowed a small satisfied smile to curve his hard mouth. True, the man he had really wanted to meet, Charles Fairfax, had died a year ago. But his family and firm still existed, and would do just as well for his purpose.

He glanced around the glittering throng. London's social élite letting their hair down in a costume ball in aid of African children, and apparently a favoured charity of the Fairfax family. The bitter irony of it did not escape him and for a moment his black eyes glinted with an unholy light.

Last December when his mother, as if sensing the end was near, had finally told him the truth about the death of his sister Suki twenty-six years ago it had given him one hell of a shock. Actually Suki had been his half-sister, but as a child he had never thought of her like that. To him she had been his older sister who took care of him.

He had believed Suki died in a car accident, tragic but unavoidable. But apparently she had deliberately driven her car off a cliff and left a note for his mother that she had immediately destroyed.

Suki had committed suicide because she had been convinced it was due to her family name and her illegitimacy that her lover, Charles Fairfax, had left her and married someone else. Then his mother had made him promise never to be ashamed of his name or his heritage.

Bitterness and bile rose in his throat just thinking about it now. He had named his company in memory of Suki, but the name had an added poignancy now. The letter he had discovered among his mother's papers after her death had confirmed she had told him the truth and more, and he had vowed on his mother's grave to avenge the insult to his sister no matter how long it took.

He was not a fan of costume parties and usually avoided them like the plague, but on this occasion he had an ulterior motive for accepting the invitation to share a table with the Fairfax family.

A deep frown marred his broad brow. Never in his hugely successful career had he ever had any trouble taking over any company he wanted and Fairfax Engineering should have been an easy acquisition. His first idea had been a hostile takeover bid and then the destruction of the company, but on studying the firm's set-up he was reluctantly forced to the conclusion that plan would not work.

The problem was the company was privately owned by family members and a small portion was diverted into a share scheme for the workforce. Also unfortunately for him it was well run and profitable. It had originally been based on the ownership of a coalmine, but a previous Fairfax had had the foresight to expand into engineering. Now that coalmining was virtually defunct in Britain the firm had found a niche market building a specific type of earth-moving equipment that was used in most countries in Europe.

With a few discreet enquiries it had become obvious none of the principal shareholders was prepared to sell even at a very generous price, and, while not giving up on a buyout, he had been obliged to adopt another strategy.

He had planned to persuade the company it would be in their best interest to expand into America and China, with his expert advice and generous financial backing, of course. Then when they had overextended themselves financially he could step in and pull the rug from under them and take the firm, in the process virtually bankrupting the Fairfax family. With that in mind he had deliberately made the acquaintance of the chairman of the board, and the MD, Tom, the son of Charles Fairfax.

The only downside to his strategy was it was taking him a hell of a lot longer than he had anticipated to grind the Fairfax name into the dust. Three months of manoeuvring and, while he was closer to attaining his goal, he wasn't there yet. The problem was the son and uncle that ran the business were both competent but very conservative businessmen and, again unfortunately for Anton, neither of them appeared to be particularly greedy or the type to take unnecessary risks.

But why would they be? he thought cynically. The company was over a hundred and sixty years old and they had never had to fight to make a living or to be accepted by their peers.

'Anton, darling, what are you thinking?'

He disliked the question, though he had heard it often enough and experience had taught him where women were concerned it was best ignored or answered with a white lie. Exasperated, he looked down at the woman in his arms. 'The latest figure on the Dow Jones—nothing that would interest you.'

'My figure is the only one you should be thinking of,' she responded with a pout, plastering herself to him.

'Save the flirting for your husband. I'm immune,' he said bluntly. Eloise was very beautiful, but she did nothing for him except remind him of his sister. That was why he had helped her out of a bad situation twelve years ago in Lima when her manager at the time had signed her up for what was undeniably a porn movie. He got her out of the contract and found her a reputable manager and they had been friends ever since. She was married to a close friend of his and yet given the chance she wasn't above trying to seduce him.

He supposed it was his own fault in a way because once, a decade ago, he had succumbed to her charms one night, though he had very quickly realized he had made a big mistake. Their friendship had survived, and now it was a game she played whenever they met, and he could not entirely blame her. He should have got tough with her long since.

Eloise was her husband's responsibility now. He had to stop pandering to her constant whims this time to hold her hand while she auditioned for a lead in a West End musical. Actually it had been no hardship because he was staying in London a lot more than he had at first anticipated. He had Fairfax Engineering firmly in his sights… He almost felt sorry for the son and daughter; they were young and no competition for him.

He thought of the report he had got from the investigator some months ago. The only photo of the daughter was of a woman standing on a deserted beach with the ocean behind her, wearing a baseball cap that masked her eyes, an oversized shirt and combat trousers. There had been no point of reference to say if she was tall or short, fat or thin.

He had been surprised when he saw her seated at the table. The photo had not done her justice. A ridiculous horned headband held back a shinning mane of blonde hair that fell smooth as silk down past her shoulder blades. Whether the colour was natural or dyed he didn't know, but it looked good. She had the peaches and cream complexion of a stereotypical English rose with magnificent big blue eyes, a full-lipped wide mouth and her breasts looked just about perfect. As for the rest he could not tell, average height maybe. But as a connoisseur of women he would reserve judgement until he saw her standing up. She could quite possibly have a big behind and short stumpy legs. Not that it concerned him; he wasn't going there. The fact she was a Fairfax was a huge turn-off; he wouldn't touch her if she were the last woman in the world.

Charles Fairfax had married the Honourable Sara Deveral in what had been the society wedding of the year twenty-six years ago. His wife had borne him a son nine months later, Tom, and a daughter, Emily, a year after that. The perfect family…

Emily Fairfax had led a charmed life. She had the best of everything. A loving family, a good education, a career of sorts as a freelance archaeologist, and she moved in London society with a confidence that was bred in the bone. The likes of Charles Fairfax were big on breeding, and the thought brought back the bitter resentment that had simmered within him since the death of his mother.

'I don't believe it.' Eloise tilted back her head and Anton glanced down at her. 'Max is actually dancing the tango...'

Anton was diverted from his sombre thoughts and followed his partner's gaze, his dark eyes widening in shock and something more as they settled on his Head of Security and erstwhile body-guard, though Max, at fifty, was more of a friend than anything else. He hadn't registered the band was playing the tango.

When Anton had a woman in his arms he held her close and naturally moved to the rhythm of the music, the steps not important. But Max was old school and was dancing the tango with all the passion and arrogance of a real aficionado. Incredibly his partner was with him every step of the way.

His eyes narrowed, absorbing the picture she presented. Emily Fairfax was stunning, and the only reason Anton had thought she was average height was instantly apparent. She had fantastically long legs in proportion to her height, a round tight behind, narrow waist and high firm breasts. The red suit was glued to her like a second skin leaving absolutely nothing to the imagination and as Max swung her around Anton doubted there was a man in the room who wasn't watching her. Her blonde hair swung around her shoulders in a shimmering cloud as she moved. And what a mover... An instant pleasurable though inconvenient sensation stirred in Anton's loins.

'Don't they look ridiculous?' Eloise tugged on his neck. 'No one dances like that these days.'

'What…? Yes…' he lied, for once less than his suave self, while silently conceding the pair looked superb, and the majority of people on the floor had stopped to watch. Max dipped Emily low over his arm, her hair touching the floor as the music drew to a close. Anton saw Emily grin as Max lifted her upright and then burst out laughing as the applause echoed around the ballroom.

The woman was not afraid of making an exhibition of herself, and, given the fire and passion in the way she danced, she was definitely no innocent. Such passion could not be confined solely to the dance floor; he recalled that she had been engaged once, according to the report he had read, and there had probably been quite a few men since.

Suddenly, having decided he would not touch her if she were the last woman on earth, Anton was imagining her long, lithesome naked body under his, and it took all his self-control to rein in his rampant libido—something that hadn't happened to him in years.

Deep in thought, he frowned as he led Eloise back to the table. He had set out to destroy Fairfax Engineering, everything Charles Fairfax owned, but he had to concede it was going to take him some time. But now an alternative scenario, a way to hedge his bet on gaining control of the company, formed in his Machiavellian mind. The solution he reached had a perfect poetic justice to it that made his firm lips twist in a brief, decidedly sinister smile.

Marriage had never appealed to him before, but he was thirty-seven, an ideal time to take a wife and produce an heir to inherit his fortune. He bred horses in Peru, and at least physically Emily Fairfax was good breeding stock, he assessed sardonically. As for her morals, he wasn't bothered about the past men in her life, with what he had on her family, she would dance

to his tune and disruption to his life would be minimal. He
frowned again; maybe Emily Fairfax had a man in her life now.
Not that he was afraid of competition—he never had any trouble
getting any woman he wanted. With his incredible wealth his
problem was the reverse: fighting them off. And Emily had no
partner with her tonight, which left him a clear field.

'Thank you, Max.' Emily was still smiling as her dancing
partner held out her chair for her. 'I really enjoyed that,' she said
as she sat down.

'It is good to see the fortune the parents spent on sending us
both to dancing classes wasn't completely wasted,' Tom said,
grinning as he and Helen sat down.

'The lessons were certainly wasted on you,' Helen quipped.
'I don't think my feet will ever recover.'

Lisa piped up with, 'Join the club—after forty years of
marriage and countless attempts at dancing James still has two
left feet.'

Emily laughed at the friendly banter between her family and
friends, unaware that the other couple had returned to the table.

CHAPTER TWO

IT WAS a shock when into the cheerful atmosphere Anton Diaz laid a hand on Emily's arm and asked her for the next dance.

She wanted to refuse, but, glancing at Max, she saw he had taken Eloise's hand and was obviously going to dance with her. The hostile look the other woman gave Anton said louder than words she wasn't delighted at the change of partner.

'Go on, Emily,' Tom encouraged. 'You know you love dancing.' He grinned. 'And if our wives are to be believed James and I are useless. Anton is your only chance.'

'Thanks, brother.' Emily snorted and reluctantly accepted and rose to her feet.

Anton gave her a wry smile. 'Your brother lacks a little subtlety,' he drawled as if he knew exactly what she was thinking. 'But I am not complaining if it gets you in my arms.'

Then, rather than taking her arm, he placed his own very firmly around her waist, his strong hand curving over her hip-bone as he urged her towards the dance floor. His touch was much too personal and his great body much too close for Emily's comfort and it only got worse...

As soon as they reached the dance floor he turned her to face him, his arm tightening around her waist as he drew her closer, and at that moment the band began playing a dreamy ballad. She stiffened in his hold, determined to resist a sudden inexplicable desire to collapse against him as he took her hand and linked his fingers with hers and cradled it against his broad chest.

'You surprised me, Emily,' he said, his dark eyes seeking hers. 'You dance the tango superbly—I was quite envious of Max,' he admitted. 'Though to be honest, dancing is not one of my talents. I could not tango to save my life. I am more a shuffle-to-the-music man,' he said with a self-effacing grin that lightened his saturnine features, making him look somewhat approachable. 'So I hope you won't be disappointed,' he concluded with a querying arch of one black brow.

Disappointed... It was a rare occurrence for Emily to dance with a man she had literally to look up to and it turned out to be frighteningly seductive. He fitted her perfectly and, enveloped in his arms, the black cloak enfolding her created an added intimacy. Disappointment was not an emotion troubling Emily, though a host of others were. With his long leg subtly easing between hers as he turned her slowly to the romantic music, her pulse raced, her heart pounded and every nerve end in her body was screaming with tension as she battled to retain control of her wayward body. The damn latex suit was no help; it simply emphasized every brush of his muscular body against hers. And she seriously doubted Anton Diaz had ever disappointed a woman in his life. Certainly not the lovely Eloise, and the thought cooled her helpless reaction to him enough for her to respond.

'Oh, I think not,' she said with blunt honesty. She knew she was reasonably attractive and she had been hit on by many men over the years, but since her failed engagement she had learnt to put men off with no trouble. 'I also think, Mr Diaz, a man of your wealth and power is perfectly well aware of his talents and exploits them quite ruthlessly for his own ends.' Anton might make her heart beat faster—her and the rest of the female population—but she had no intention of falling for his charm. 'As I'm sure the tabloids and your friend Eloise could confirm,' she ended dryly.

'Ah, Emily, you have been listening to gossip. What was it? I was brought up in a brothel surrounded by willing women,' he mocked. 'Sorry to disappoint, but it is not true, though my grandmother did own one,' he admitted, 'and it is a poor reflection on the male of the species that she made rather a lot of money. Enough to send her daughter to the best school in the country and on to a finishing school in Switzerland.'

Emily's blue eyes widened in surprise at his blunt revelations, her tension forgotten as she listened intrigued as he continued.

'When she was in Europe she met and fell in love with a Greek man who was unfortunately married with children. But he was decent enough to set her up in a house in Corinth where I was born. Their affair lasted for years, he died when I was twelve and my mother decided to return to Peru.'

'That is so sad. Your poor mother, you poor boy,' she murmured. Totally absorbed in his story, she compassionately squeezed his hand.

'I might have guessed you would feel sorry for me.' His dark head bent and his lips brushed her brow. 'Ah, Emily, you are so naive and so misguided. As a wealthy man's mistress my mother was never poor in the monetary sense and neither was I.' He looked into her big blue eyes, his own gleaming with cynical amusement. 'I hate to disillusion you, but your sympathy is wasted on me.'

'So why did you tell me all that?' she asked, puzzled. He did not strike her as the sort of man who would bare his soul to a relative stranger.

'Maybe because it got you to relax in my arms.' He smiled.

'Was it all lies?' she shot back, her body stiffening again, this time in anger.

'Not all…I actually am a bastard.' He grinned, the hand at her waist stroking slowly up her back, drawing her closer still. And she involuntarily trembled in his hold. 'And as you so rightly said,' he drawled softly, 'I use all the talents I have to get what I want. And I want you, Emily Fairfax.'

Stunned by his outrageous comment, she stared up into his night-black eyes, and saw the desire he made no attempt to hide. 'You devious devil,' she exclaimed.

'Angel,' he amended, his dark head dipping, his warm breath tickling her ear as he urged her hard against him, making her intimately aware of his aroused state. 'And the way you tremble in my arms I know you want me. The attraction between us was instant and electric so don't pretend otherwise, Emily,' he commanded, and straightened up.

'You're unbelievable,' she gasped. Though she could not deny the trembling, or the attraction, she had no intention of succumbing to such blatant seduction. 'Coming on to me when you have the beautiful Eloise with—'

He cut her off. 'Eloise is a very old friend, nothing more I can assure you, and so could her husband,' he said, his dark eyes holding hers, a wicked gleam in their ebony depths. 'She is quite a famous television star in Latin America, but she has ambitions to be famous worldwide. Which is why she is over here to discuss the possibility of starring in a musical production in the West End next year. She is going back to her husband tomorrow so you have nothing to be jealous about.'

'Jealous. Are you crazy? I don't even know you,' Emily spluttered.

'That is soon remedied. I will call you tomorrow and arrange a time for our dinner date,' he declared, and stopped dancing, his hands sliding to span her waist, and hold her still. 'But now I think we'd better get back to the table, before people start to gossip. The music has ended.'

Emily had not noticed, and, embarrassed, she followed him like a lamb to slaughter, she realized later…much later…

'For heaven's sake, Emily, will you stop devouring that disgusting fry-up—it is turning my stomach—and listen to me,' Helen declared. 'You have to put the poor man out of his misery and have dinner with him. He has sent you roses every single day and the housekeeper is fed up with taking his phone calls. The house is overflowing with blooms and in my pregnant state I might very well get hay fever.'

Emily popped the last bit of fried egg into her mouth, chewed, then grinned at her sister-in-law. 'You know the solution—I told you to throw the flowers away. I'm not interested.'

'Liar—the woman is not born who would not fancy Anton Diaz. Your trouble is you're afraid to get involved after the hateful Nigel. You haven't dated any man for more than a couple of weeks in years.'

'*Moi*?' Emily quipped, placing a hand on her heart. 'I am not afraid of anyone, but I know a devil when I see one, and Anton Diaz is not the kind of man any sensible woman would ever get involved with.'

'Forget the sensible, and live a little. You're at home for the next few months and your research at the museum does not take more than a couple of days a week. It is spring, when a young woman's fancy turns to love.'

'A young man's fancy, you mean, and Anton Diaz is no young man,' Emily responded dryly.

'So what if he is a dozen or more years older than you? You

have plenty of spare time and a wild passionate affair with an experienced man would do you the world of good.'

'I don't think so, and I have no time right now. I am going to view another apartment today,' Emily said, hoping to change the subject, because the subject of Anton Diaz had taken up a great deal of her waking thoughts since the night she had met him. His phone calls she had refused after the first day as just the sound of his deep accented voice made her temperature rise and her whole body blush; the daily roses she could do nothing about.

'Oh, for heaven's sake, Emily, forget about buying an apartment. It's a stupid idea. This is your family home, has been for generations since the first Fairfax made his fortune as a coal baron in the nineteenth century, and it is big enough for all of us and half a dozen more.'

Helen rolled her eyes around the spacious breakfast room of the ten-bedroomed double-fronted Georgian house in the heart of Kensington. 'I would hate it if you left and you would hate living on your own. Admit it. And you might as well admit you fancy Anton Diaz something rotten. I have seen the way you try not to blush every time his name is mentioned. You can't fool me.'

Emily groaned. 'Your trouble is, Helen, you know me far too well.' She rose to her feet and smiled wryly down at her sister-in-law. 'I am still going to look at the apartment, though. After all, if I am going to have a wild, passionate affair I will need a place of my own. I'm sure you wouldn't appreciate my bringing a lover back here where your gorgeous child might see and hear more than she should.' She grinned.

'You're going to do it—you're going out with the man?'

'Maybe if Anton calls again and asks me out I will accept. Satisfied?'

'You will accept what?' Tom demanded as he walked into the room, with his daughter in his arms.

'Emily is going out with Anton Diaz,' Helen declared.

'Is that wise, sis?' he asked Emily, his blue eyes serious as they rested on her. 'He is a hell of a lot older than you. Are you sure you know what you are doing? Don't get me wrong, he is a great guy and his business knowledge is second to none—his input and advice to Fairfax Engineering has been exceptional. But he is the type of man that makes other men want to lock up their wives and daughters. The man definitely lives in the fast lane and has a poor track record with women.'

'I don't believe it!' Emily exclaimed. 'Much as I love you two, you should work at coordinating your opinions and advice.' And, grinning, she walked out.

Fate, kismet, whatever it was, but as she entered the hall the telephone rang and she answered. Anton...

'You're a very hard lady to get hold of, Emily. But I like a challenge. Have dinner with me tonight?'

So, she did what she had wanted to do for days and said yes...

Emily viewed the apartment and decided against it. Then spent the rest of the morning at the museum, and the afternoon shopping for a new dress.

Emily smiled, happy with her reflection in the mirror, and, straightening her shoulders, she picked up her dark blue wrap and matching purse from the bed and left the room. She was nervous, butterflies were fluttering in her stomach, but none of her inner emotions showed as she opened the drawing-room door and walked in. Anton Diaz was picking her up at seven and it was ten to.

'Well, Helen, will I do?' She smiled at her sister-in-law reclining on a sofa, a glass of juice in her hand, and saw the embarrassed expression on her face just as a deep dark voice responded.

'You look beautiful, Emily.'

Emily turned her head, her eyes widening as Anton walked towards her from the far side of the room, Tom trailing in his wake.

'Thank you.' She accepted the compliment politely, but it was an effort. She had thought he looked dangerous dressed as a dark angel, but in a perfectly tailored light grey suit with a white shirt and silk tie he looked gorgeous. 'You're early,' she added, raising her eyes to his face. He had stopped barely a foot from her, and his dark gaze slid slowly over her from head to toe, then he lifted his eyes to hers and what she saw in the smouldering black depths made the breath catch in her throat.

For the second time in a week Anton Diaz could not control his instant arousal at the sight of a woman. He had seen a photo of Emily in baggy clothes, and seen her in a very sexy latex suit with her hair down. But the Emily who stood before him now was something else again. She was the personification of sophisticated elegance.

Her blonde hair was swept up into a knot on top of her head, her make-up understated, but perfect. Her big blue eyes were accentuated even more by the clever use of cosmetics, her full lips a soft glossy rose. As for her gown, it was designer; he had bought enough over the years to know. Ice-blue to match her eyes, it was cut on the bias, the bodice, supported by slight straps, clung faithfully to her high firm breasts and subtly shaped her narrow waist and hips to flare ever so slightly a few inches from the hem that ended on her knees. Not too short to appear tacky, but short enough for a man to fantasize about slipping his hand beneath it.

'Beautiful does not do you justice—you look exquisite, Emily. I will be the envy of every man in the restaurant.' Reaching for a cashmere wrap that she held in her hand, he gently took it and slipped it over her shoulders. 'Shall we go?'

It was definitely going to be no hardship to bed the lovely Emily, the finer details of when and where were all he had to decide on, he thought as he battled to control his libido.

Amazingly, Tom Fairfax, despite his usual easygoing nature, had taken him to one side when he had arrived and told him quite seriously he expected Anton to behave himself with Emily and return her home at a reasonable hour. No one had attempted to tell him what to do in years, if ever, and he had been too stunned to reply when Emily had walked into the room.

He could understand the man's concern, but it simply reminded him that he had been unable to take care of his own sister, and the memory cooled his wayward body in an instant.

Emily was too flustered to do more than take the hand Anton offered her. She felt his hand tighten on hers, and caught a flicker of some strange emotion in his dark eyes, gone as he turned and said goodnight to Tom and Helen.

He opened the passenger door of a silver Bentley and ushered her inside. She watched as he walked around the bonnet and slid behind the wheel. He glanced at her, one brow arched enquiringly, and she realized she was staring like a besotted fool.

'Where are you taking me?' She blurted the first thing that came into her head.

He chuckled a deep dark sound. 'To dinner, Emily.' Slipping a hand around her neck, he tilted her face to his dark eyes dancing with amusement. 'But ultimately to my bed.'

His provocative statement had her lips parting in a shocked gasp, and Anton's mouth covered them, firm, warm and tender. Her lips tingled and trembled as his hand trailed around her throat, his fingers curving around her small chin to hold her firm as the tip of his tongue sought hers with an eroticism that ignited a sudden warmth deep inside her. Her eyes closed and her hands slid up to clasp his nape, her fingers trailing involuntarily into the silken blackness of his hair as he deepened the kiss, his tongue probing the moist interior of her mouth, and the slow-burning heat ignited into flame.

'Emily.' He raised his head, and lifted her hands from their death-like grip around his neck. 'Emily, we have to go.'

She looked dazedly up at him, then down at his hands holding hers. Had she really flung her arms around him and clung like a limpet? And suddenly the heat of arousal became the heat of embarrassment.

'What did you do that for?' she asked.

'I believe in getting the first kiss over with quickly, instead of wondering all evening, and to be blunt you have kept me waiting a week already.' He grinned.

'I'm surprised you persisted.' She grinned back, suddenly feeling wonderful, all her doubts and fears about Anton wiped out by his kiss.

'I surprised myself. I am of the W.C. Fields train of thought. If at first you don't succeed, try, try, and then give up—there is no point in being a damn fool about it. Usually two approaches with no response and I move on. But in your case I made an exception. You should be flattered.'

Emily chuckled. 'You are impossibly arrogant, Anton.'

'Yes, but you like me.' He grinned and started the car.

The restaurant was exclusive, the food superb and Anton the perfect dinner companion. His conversation was witty and gradually she relaxed. He told her he spent a lot of time travelling between his head office in New York, and the subsidiaries in Sydney, London and Athens, where he had an island villa within commuting distance by helicopter. But he tried to spend the winter months on his estate in Peru.

Without being aware of it, Emily was already half in love with him by the time he took her home.

'Admit it, Emily, you enjoyed yourself tonight,' Anton prompted as he stopped the car outside her home and turned to look at her. 'I am not quite the ogre you thought, hmm?' And he slid an arm around her shoulders.

'I concede you really are very civilized and, yes, I did enjoy myself.' The champagne she had consumed making her ever so slightly tipsy, she smiled up at him and added, 'But you are still arrogant.'

'Maybe, but will you allow me to take you out again tomorrow night?' he asked formally, but there was nothing formal about the sensual gleam in the black depths of the eyes that held hers as he drew her close.

'Yes,' she murmured, and watched in helpless anticipation as his dark head bent and his wide mouth covered hers.

The second kiss was even better than the first and she leant into him with bone-melting enthusiasm, her arms eagerly wrapping around his neck. She felt his great body tense, felt the brush of one hand against the fabric covering her breast as he deepened the kiss, his tongue searching her mouth with a skilful eroticism that sent shuddering sensations of pure pleasure coursing hotly through her slender body.

She inhaled the unique masculine scent of him, trembled with wild excitement at the pleasure of his kiss, a kiss so deep, so passionate, she never wanted to come up for air. When his fingers closed around the strap of her dress she quivered, but made no objection as he peeled the fabric down over her braless breasts.

He raised his head and she didn't understand his husky

words as he palmed her breast, his long fingers grazing over the rosy tip. Her whole body jerked and her head fell back as he lowered his head and his mouth closed over an exposed nipple. Fierce sensations lanced from her breasts to her loins, moisture pooling between her thighs. She groaned out loud as with tongue and teeth he teased her rigid nipples, until she was a quivering mass of heated sensations she had never experienced before, never believed existed until now.

She threaded her hands through his dark hair, and held him to her aching body, wanting more. She felt the gentle trail of his strong hand sliding beneath her skirt, stroking up the silken smoothness of her thigh, felt his long fingers trace the thin strip of lace between her legs. Involuntarily her legs parted and one long finger edged beneath her panties.

'My God!' Anton exclaimed, rearing back. 'What the hell am I doing?'

She stared up at him, her body sprawled back against the seat in total abandonment, her blue eyes glittering wildly and her pale skin flushed with the heat of arousal at the hands of a man for the first time in her twenty-four years. Quickly he smoothed her skirt down over her thighs and hauled her up in the seat, slipping the straps of her dress back over her shoulder, and placing her wrap carefully around her, folding it over her still-tingling breasts.

'That's better,' he said, his dark eyes suddenly shadowed.

Emily's body still pulsed with sensation, but slowly it dawned on her Anton was no way near as affected.

'Sorry, Emily, I never meant to take things so far in the car of all places.' He smoothed a few tendrils of hair from her brow. 'Damn it to hell, I promised your brother I would look after you.' He swore.

That did get through to Emily. 'You promised my brother...'

she exclaimed. 'You mean Tom had the nerve… I'll kill him.'
She could not believe her own brother, and her embarrassment
at her helpless capitulation to Anton was overtaken by her
anger at Tom. 'He seems to forget I am a grown woman and
perfectly able to look after myself.'

'I'm sure you are,' Anton agreed. 'But right now you better
get indoors, before I lose control completely,' he added with a
self-derisory grimace as he got out of the car and walked around
to open the passenger door. He slipped an arm around her waist
and led her to the imposing front door of her home. 'I won't
come in, I don't dare.' Dropping a swift kiss on the top of her
head, he added, 'I'll call you in the morning.' He waited as
Emily, her head in a whirl of chaotic emotions—embarrassment, anger and, most telling of all, frustration—found her
key, opened the door and walked in.

CHAPTER THREE

THE weeks that followed were like a fairy tale to Emily. She was head over heels in love with Anton Diaz. The love she had thought she had felt for Nigel was nothing compared to how Anton made her feel. There was no point in denying it. She only had to hear his deep, melodious accented voice to go weak at the knees, and when he touched her excitement buzzed through every nerve in her body. She wanted him in ways she had never dreamed of before, but now kept her hot and restless in bed at night.

Thinking about that first night now, four weeks later, as she sat in front of the dressing mirror applying her make-up, ignited a slow-burning heat in the pit of Emily's stomach. But then that was something that pretty much happened every time she thought of Anton these days. A secretive smile curved her full lips as she ran a brush through her hair and rose to her feet.

Anton had been in New York for almost a week, and she ached to see him again. In fact she ached for him, because for some reason there had been no repeat of that first steamy episode except in her head.

They had enjoyed themselves over a few dinners and a trip to the theatre. She had accompanied him on several high-profile social occasions that included his business acquaintances, and the one time they had attended a film première he had quite proudly confirmed to the waiting photographers that they were an item.

But it was their relationship on the sexual front that puzzled Emily. Innocent though she was, she knew deep in her heart she wanted him with every fibre of her being. Given his reputation, she knew the best she could hope for was an affair, and she had confidently expected to be invited to his London penthouse. Within a week of meeting him, she had prepared for their relationship to progress to the physical, but it had not advanced at all. On the contrary, Anton had never even suggested taking her to his apartment, and made a point of drawing back after a kiss or two, while she was left aching for more…

Still, perhaps after a six-day separation tomorrow night would be the night, she thought as she clipped the diamond studs in her ears and stood back to view her reflection. But first she had to get through tonight. A family party for her uncle Sir Clive Deveral's birthday.

Her mother's brother was a bachelor and it was a bit of a tradition that he dined with them all on his birthday before heading off later to his club and his old navy mates to reminisce and get drunk. She had made a determined effort to dress up for her uncle because she knew he really appreciated glamorous women.

He had told her so when, in his own bumbling way, he had tried to comfort her after her disastrous engagement. He had confided that years ago he had lost his fiancée to another man, but he had soon got over it; with so many glamorous women to choose from he preferred to play the field. Then realizing what he had said, he had exclaimed, 'Not that I mean you should play the field. Heaven forbid. I simply meant there are plenty more fish in the sea,' and made her laugh.

He was a real sweetie and Emily adored him. She had spent

many a school holiday at his home, Deveral Hall in Lincolnshire, or at his rather dilapidated villa in Corfu. When her childhood dreams of being a ballerina were dashed by her increasing height it was her uncle who had taught her never to waste time hankering after things that she could not change and move on. Then he had got her interested in archaeology and sailing and swimming in the warm waters off the Greek island and had been instrumental in her decision to be a marine archaeologist.

She smiled at her image in the mirror. The dress she wore was a strapless silver lamé that clung to every inch of her body like a second skin to end six inches above her knees. She had left her long hair loose and she was wearing ridiculously high-heeled diamanté sandals that showed off her legs to the max.

Emily was still smiling to herself as she walked down the stairs to join the family for pre-dinner drinks. Her uncle would love her outfit—he was always telling her that the latest generation of men on the Fairfax side of the family needed shocking out of their staid conservatism once in a while. For that reason he always turned up at any family dinner in a velvet dinner jacket and outrageous waistcoats. The rest of the family would probably have a fit.

She reached the bottom of the stairs and headed towards the sound of talk and laughter coming from the drawing room, and then turned again as the doorbell rang.

'I'll get it, Mindy,' she said as the flustered housekeeper popped out of the kitchen.

She opened the door and her mouth fell open with shock. 'Anton, what are you doing here? I thought you weren't due back until tomorrow.'

'Obviously I got back not a minute too soon.' His dark eyes glittered with some fierce emotion as they swept over her. 'You look unbelievable, though I find it hard to believe you dressed like that for an evening at home. Who is my competition?' he demanded, his dark eyes narrowing with anger on her face. Then without a word he hauled her into his arms and covered her mouth with his own in a hard possessive kiss that knocked the breath from her body.

When he finally allowed her to breathe again she looked up into his burning black eyes. 'What was that for?' she gasped.

'To remind you, you are mine. Now who is he?'

'You're jealous—you think I am going out with another man,' Emily prompted, ridiculously delighted, and, lifting a finger, she stroked the firm line of his jaw. 'You have no need to be, Anton. There is no other man, and we are having a birthday party for my uncle,' she explained, a broad smile curving her slightly swollen lips. 'Come and join us. You will make the dinner table up to an even number.' And she watched as what looked surprisingly like a blush stained his high cheekbones.

'What can I say?' He groaned, holding her away from him. 'Except I've missed you.' His eyes roamed hungrily over her and then, grabbing her arm, he urged her inside. 'I have to speak to Tom.'

'Why?'

'I want to marry you, and I need to ask his permission.'

'What?'

'You heard.' He folded her against his long body. 'Marry me, Emily. I can't wait any longer.'

Not the most romantic proposal in the world, but Emily's blue eyes filled with tears of happiness. Suddenly everything made sense. Anton, wonderful Anton, the man she loved with all her heart, the man she had been worrying would never take her to bed, actually wanted to marry her. Now his behaviour made magnificent sense. She had heard the rumours of his many mistresses, but with her he had behaved with admirable restraint because he wanted more, he wanted her to be his wife, he loved her.

'Yes, oh, yes,' she cried, and flung her arms around his neck.

'What is going on out here?'

Anton raised his eyes and looked at Tom over the top of Emily's head. He had shocked himself by proposing marriage so precipitously. He had had it all planned, the ring in his pocket, a romantic dinner, a skilful seduction; instead he had blurted it out in the doorway like an idiot. But hell! If ever a woman looked like sex on legs and ready to bed it was Emily tonight, he reasoned, so naturally he had to get in quick. And Emily had said yes, mission accomplished. Not that he had doubted for a moment she would say yes, and he refused to admit it was the thought of Emily seeing another man that was responsible for his hasty proposal. He straightened his broad shoulders and tightened his arm around Emily's waist.

'I have just asked Emily to marry me, Tom, and she has agreed. But we would like your blessing,' he said, once more in complete control.

'Is this true, Emily? Is Anton the man for you?' Tom asked quietly, his eyes on his sister.

'Oh, yes.'

'In that case you have my blessing.' Anton met his soon-to-be brother-in-law's eyes and saw the slight reservation in the blue depths. 'But you are a lot older than Emily.' For that, read *You have a reputation with women*, Anton understood instantly. 'And if you hurt her in any way you will have me to answer to.'

'I'll guard her with my life,' Anton declared, and he meant it, though not necessarily for the reason Tom Fairfax thought...

'Knowing Emily and given her career choice, I don't envy you,' Tom teased.

'Tom—please…' Emily groaned. 'You are going to put Anton off before I get the ring on my finger.'

'Never.' Anton glanced down at the woman by his side. 'As your husband I will support you every which way you want, Emily.'

'So stop making cow's eyes at her, and come and meet the rest of the family.' Tom grinned. 'We can make it a double celebration and you will have some idea of what you are getting into, my friend.'

Anton knew exactly what he was getting into, he had engineered the whole thing, so he was surprised that he actually felt something suspiciously like guilt as the introductions were made. Tom and Helen, he knew of course, and James and Lisa Browning. The Brownings' two adult sons and their wives seemed pleasant enough. Another aunt, Jane, was the younger sister of Sara Fairfax, a widow with twin sons about twenty. Then there was the birthday boy, Sir Clive Deveral, wearing a deep blue velvet dinner jacket, a ruffled yellow shirt and a brilliant scarlet waistcoat with a face to match.

Although he had seen all their names on the report his investigator had presented, meeting them in the flesh was a little disconcerting. As the dinner progressed he found it impossible to dislike them. Everyone without exception made him welcome and congratulated him on having won Emily's hand in marriage. The conversation was lively and funny and inevitably reminiscences of other family parties were laughed over. For the first time in years he wondered if there was something to be said for a large close-knit family.

'So what did you think of them?' Emily asked Anton, her arm linked in his as she walked him to the door at one in the morning.

'I think your uncle Clive is deliberately outrageous but a great character and the rest are all lovely just like you,' he murmured as he slipped his hand in his pocket and withdrew a small velvet box.

Emily stared in wonder and a happiness so profound she could not speak.

'I meant to do this over a romantic dinner for two.' His lips quirked at the corners in a wry smile as he opened the box. 'But events rather overtook us.' And grasping her hand, he raised it to his lips and pressed a soft kiss on the backs of her fingers, before sliding a magnificent sapphire and diamond ring onto her finger.

Tears of joy sparkled in Emily's eyes as she looked up into his darkly handsome face. 'It is beautiful. I love it and I love you,' she declared. Anton was everything she wanted, and the fact he had said in front of Tom he would support her in her career banished the faintest doubt, and she kissed him.

They were married quietly on a Wednesday a month later in the church adjacent to her uncle Clive's home, Deveral Hall. Uncle Clive considered Tom and Emily as close to his own children as he would ever get and was delighted to throw open his once elegant but now slightly shabby home for the occasion.

On a brilliant day in late May the old stone house glowed mellowly in the sun. Emily was a vision in white and Anton every inch the perfect groom, tall, dark and strikingly attractive. The fifty-odd guests, mostly family and friends of Emily, were all agreed it was a wonderful intimate wedding.

Anton stared down at his sleeping bride, a slow satisfied smile curving his firm lips, his dark eyes gleaming with triumph.

Emily Fairfax was his... His wife...Señora Diaz...or Mrs...whatever. He considered himself a citizen of the world, and it was only the Diaz that was important. He had applied

for a passport weeks ago in her married name, and on production of the wedding certificate Max pulled a few strings and
obtained the new passport and delivered it as they boarded the
plane for Monte Carlo. Anton had accomplished what he had
set out to do from the first time he had set eyes on her. He had
married Charles Fairfax's daughter, the niece of a knight of the
realm. Not that he cared about titles, but Charles Fairfax certainly had.

Anton's expression darkened. According to his mother, over
twenty-six years ago Charles Fairfax had been on holiday in
Greece and had seduced Anton's eighteen-year-old sister, Suki.
Anton had been eleven at the time and attending boarding
school so had known nothing about it. When his sister had died
a few months later in a car accident he had been devastated, but
it was only after his mother had died he had pieced together the
full extent of Charles Fairfax's betrayal, from the letter ad-
dressed to Suki he had found among his mother's things.

Charles Fairfax had left Suki pregnant and returned to
London. When she had contacted him about the child he had
written back saying he did not believe the child was his. Then
added he was well aware that Suki was the illegitimate daughter
of a Frenchman, and that her mother was the daughter of a
Peruvian brothel-keeper, and was now the mistress of a wealthy
Greek and had yet another illegitimate child. With such a
pedigree there was no way, even if he were free, which he was
not, that the proud old name of Fairfax would ever be associated
with the name Diaz.

Five months after Fairfax had left her, Suki had picked up a
copy of *The Times* newspaper and read the announcement of
the wedding of Charles Fairfax to Sir Clive Thomas Deveral's
sister, Sara Deveral, and she had given up all hope and committed suicide. Killing herself and her unborn child.

Anton shook his head to dispel the dark memories. Today he had righted the wrong done to his family in a way he knew his mother would have appreciated. Emily Fairfax was now a Diaz, a very fitting revenge.

As for Emily, he glanced back at her sleeping form in the seat beside him. She really was exquisite; in fact, if he had met her without the past to consider, while he would not have married her, he would certainly have bedded her and kept her as his mistress until he tired of her. But looking at her now with her silken blonde hair falling loosely over one side of her face, her soft lips slightly pouted in sleep, he was glad he had.

Emily was intelligent, well educated with a career of sorts and she was not likely to interfere in how he ran his life. Certainly not after he told her why he had married her, and the thought made him pause. Somehow the revenge he had achieved did not give him quite as much pleasure as he had expected. The soul-corroding bitterness that had consumed him since his mother's death had faded slightly. Probably because of Emily—she really was delightful.

Her constant avowals of love, rather than irritating him, he was beginning to find quite addictive. He had known a few women, and he was realistic enough to recognize that, great sex aside, the biggest part of his attraction was his wealth. Personally he thought love was an excuse the female of the species, Emily included, used to justify having sex with a man. Wryly he amended that thought, with the exception of the three generations of females in his family who had imagined themselves in love and suffered for it.

His grandmother had been the daughter of a wealthy Spanish Peruvian rancher, a Señor Sebastian Emanuel Diaz. Her father had disowned her after she had disgraced the family by getting pregnant and running away to Lima with a ranch hand. They never married and he left her when their daughter was barely a year old. His own mother had repeated the same mistake twice over, first by falling in love with a Frenchman who had left her with a baby girl, and then with Anton's father, a Greek who was married, and she became his mistress. While not a complete tragedy, his mother had not made the wisest of choices. As for his sister—to kill herself for love didn't bear thinking about.

No, if love existed then it was a destructive emotion and not one Anton was prepared to embrace. He lusted after Emily, but he had no illusions about the female of the species. He knew his wealth and power were probably just as much an aphrodisiac to Emily as they had been to the countless other women he had known.

The wedding had gone perfectly and they were now on his private jet heading for the South of France to board his yacht anchored off Monaco.

His dark eyes narrowed as they roamed over her lovely face, serene in sleep. He noted the fantastic sweep of her lashes over her eyes, the sensuously curved passionate mouth, the slight curve of her breasts revealed between the lapels of the wild blue silk suit she wore, and his body tightened.

Pity he had not been able to remove the exquisite white wedding gown. The image of her as he had turned to watch her walk down the aisle would live in his mind for ever. Beautiful was an understatement; her sparkling blue eyes had met his and for a long moment he had not been able to breathe, such was her effect on him. Even now remembering made his heart beat faster and he fought the temptation to kiss her awake. He had waited this long, he could wait a little longer until they reached the comfort of his yacht. He did not want to rush what he had promised himself would be a long night of passion.

A light flashed in the gathering darkness, and he heard the sudden change in the engine noise; they would be landing soon. Good, he was getting impatient. He could not remember the last time he had waited so long for a woman, if ever…though it had all been part of his plan.

Emily was a passionate woman, and as an experienced man of the world and a skilful lover Anton had recognized that immediately. He had quickly decided his best policy was to give her just a taste of what she wanted and no more. To build up her frustration until she was so desperate to have him she would accept his proposal of marriage without a second thought. Which of course she had.

Anton shifted uncomfortably in his seat. The trouble was he had suffered just as much if not more from the enforced celibacy, as the stirring in his groin could testify. He had ended his last affair a month after his mother's death when the woman he was involved with at the time had started hinting at marriage now he was alone in the world. He grimaced painfully. He had never gone so long without sex since he was a teenager, but thankfully the wait would soon be over.

A slight frown creased his brow as, thinking back over the past few weeks, he suddenly realized every time he had stopped after a kiss or two Emily had looked at him with desire-dazed eyes, and yet she had made no attempt to seduce him, no attempt to touch him intimately. Not the usual reaction of a sexually sophisticated woman. In his experience they normally made their desire very clear. Odd…or maybe not so odd, he corrected cynically. She had probably been playing the same waiting game as he had to make sure of getting a ring on her finger…

'Anton.' A throaty murmur had his eyes flying back to her face.

'You're awake. Good.' He lowered his head to taste the soft

sweetness of her luscious mouth. 'We are landing soon,' he murmured, lifting his head, and, taking her hands in his, he folded them on her lap. 'Another half-hour and we will be on board the yacht.'

'It can't be too soon.' Emily smiled up at him, her brilliant blue eyes dazzling him. 'My love. My husband.'

'I agree, wife.' Anton smiled back. Yes, she was his wife, he had succeeded, he thought complacently as, with a sexy Emily firmly clasped to his side, he led her off the jet to the waiting helicopter.

His mother must be smiling down on him and that snobbish swine Charles Fairfax must be spinning in his grave, or burning in hell. He didn't care which. Because his daughter was now a Diaz, the name he thought not fit to be connected to Fairfax. A result all around…

His hand tightened possessively around her slender waist and in that moment he decided… Actually there was no pressing need to tell Emily what a two-timing dirty swine her father was, the real reason he had married her. It was enough for Anton to know he had kept the vow he had made on his mother's grave.

Emily staggered out of the helicopter into Anton's arms. He swung her off her feet and she wrapped her arms around his neck as, ducking his head under the still-swirling blades, he carried her to the stairs leading down from the helipad and into the body of the yacht. He didn't stop until he reached the main salon and lowered her slowly to her feet.

'Welcome aboard.' He grinned down at her and Emily registered the swell of his arousal as he dipped his head and kissed her.

She felt the earth move, or maybe it was just the yacht, but either way she flung her arms around Anton's neck again and clung.

'I want to make it to the bed at least,' she heard him groan, his hands roaming restlessly down her spine and over her bottom.

Emily shivered with excitement and, glancing around her in awe, she laughed out loud. 'This is huge!' she exclaimed, turning back to Anton, and saw his lips twitch. 'I have been on expeditions on ships half this size.'

'Emily—stop talking,' Anton commanded, his ego slightly deflated. His lips sought hers once again, and she closed her eyes in willing surrender as his tongue slipped between her softly parted lips in a long drugging kiss.

Finally when she was breathless he raised his head. 'I have waited too long for this.' He peeled off his jacket and hers as he walked her backwards in what she hoped was the direction of the master cabin.

She felt her breasts swell as his hand stroked one lace-covered breast, his thumb grazing the tip over the fine fabric, and her nipples tightened into hard pulsing points of pleasure. His mouth caught her soft gasp of delight, then moments later he nudged a door open with his shoulder.

She barely registered the bedroom; she had eyes for nothing but Anton.

Without a word he cupped her face and bent his dark head, covering her mouth with his at first tenderly. Then, as she opened her mouth to him, with a fast-growing passion that she returned with helpless fervour.

'Emily.' He said her name, and, lifting his head, he locked his dark eyes with hers, black with a hunger, a passion, that burned through to her bones. His hand slid around her back to dispense with her bra and stayed to hold her to him. For a long moment he simply stared and just his gaze on her naked breasts made her tremble with excitement.

'Exquisite,' he murmured throatily as he lowered his head

to trace the slender length of her neck with his mouth and suck on the rapidly beating pulse there. Then trail lower to her breast.

His tongue licked one pert nipple and the tightened tip engorged at his touch. She cried out as his teeth gently tugged, and her head fell back over his arm, her back arching in spontaneous response as she offered herself up to the incredible pleasure only Anton could arouse. He suckled first one and then the other with a skill that drove her crazy with need and had her writhing in his hold.

She felt her skirt slide to the floor, and suddenly he was swinging her up in his arms again and lowering her gently to the bed. She whimpered as he straightened up and looked down at her.

'You have no idea how much I want you,' he grated, his black eyes ablaze as he divested himself of his clothes in seconds.

She stared at the wide tanned shoulders, the muscular, slightly hair-roughened chest, the strong hips, the powerful thighs and long legs. Totally naked and fully aroused he was almost frightening in his masculine beauty, and nervously she crossed her arms over her throbbing breasts.

'Let me look at you,' he growled and, leaning over her, he grasped the top of her minuscule lace briefs. 'All of you.' He slid them down her long legs and dropped them. Then his hands curled around her ankles and slowly stroked up her long legs tracing the curve of her hips, the indentation of her waist. She was trembling all over by the time he reached for her wrists and, unfolding her arms from her chest, pinned her hands either side of her body.

'There is no need to pretend shyness,' he husked. 'You are exquisite, more than I ever dreamed of.'

Excitement arced through her like an electric charge, her blue eyes as bright as sapphires as his dark eyes dropped to her breasts and lingered before roaming over her from head to toe once more. Emily had thought she might be embarrassed naked for the first time before Anton, but instead she was wildly excited, her slender body reacting heatedly to his intense scrutiny.

'I can't take my eyes off you, Emily, my wife. And soon to be my wife in every way.' Taking protection from a bedside table, he lowered himself down beside her, his magnificent body sliding against her, flesh on flesh.

What followed was so outside anything Emily had ever imagined it was unreal. The odd time she had imagined the act of love she had thought it would be some magical meeting of heart, body and soul, sweet, tender love reaching a joyous climax. But the violent emotions flooding through her were nothing like that.

'You can touch me, Emily,' he murmured, his dark eyes gleaming down into hers as his mouth covered hers. She reached for him in an almost desperate haste, the masculine scent of him, the sleek slide of his skin against hers, the devouring passion of his mouth igniting a white-hot heat inside her.

With tentative hands she explored the width of his shoulders, the strong spine. She shuddered as his dark head lowered and found her pouting breasts once more. No longer tentative, but eager, she stroked up his back and raked her fingers through the black silken hair of his head, holding him to her. She groaned out loud as he lifted his head and moaned her delight as he found her mouth again. The sensuality of his kiss made her head spin and her body burn.

She closed her eyes and savoured the slight masculine scent of him, and wreathed helplessly as his hands slid down the length of her body caressing, stroking and finally settling between her parted thighs.

His long fingers found the moist, hot centre of her femininity and a low aching moan escaped her, and she wanted more, much more, her hips lifting, her whole body throbbing. She was helplessly in thrall to the wonder of his expertise and her own uninhibited response. She clutched desperately at him and looked up into his taut dark face, saw the black passion in his eyes and revelled in it.

Wild and wanton, she caught his hair and pulled his head back to her mouth. She was panting with frustration and an incredible need to feel all of his long, hard body over her, in her, joined with hers. She groaned as he paused to slip on protection and then kissed her. The sensuous pressure of his lips, the thrusting of his tongue mimicking the sexual act and the fire in her blood turned her whole body into a flame of pure sensation. He settled between her thighs, and she cried his name, burning with a fever for more. His hands on her hips tightened and she arched up as he thrust home.

Emily felt a stab of pain and winced. She saw the shock in his dark eyes as he stilled and began to withdraw. But she could not let him go, not now as the thick fullness of him made her inner muscles clench, and instinctively she locked her legs around his waist, slid her arms around his back. 'Please. Please. I want you. I love you.'

She heard the sharp intake of his breath, felt the heavy beating of his heart and the tension in every muscle of his body. Then he moved, slowly thrusting a little deeper, and then withdrawing and sliding deeper still.

Miraculously her silken sheath stretched to accommodate him, and Emily was lost to everything except the pure physical wonder of his possession. The indescribable sensations beating through her, the sleek skin beneath her fingers, and the heated scent of two bodies joined. The wonder as in seconds she matched the rhythm he set, driving her ever higher to some unknown destination she ached…was dying for.

Her nails dug deep into his satin-smooth skin as great waves of ecstasy rippled through her and then roared as he thrust hard and fast and she cried out as her body convulsed in exquisite rapture, and she was flung into a hot, mindless oblivion. She heard Anton groan, and she forced her eyes open and felt his great body buck and shudder with the force of his own release.

Loosely she wrapped her arms around him as he buried his head on her shoulder. The heavy pounding of his heart against hers and his weight were a solid reminder of the power and passion, the love he had given her. A soft smile curved her lips. Anton truly was her husband.

CHAPTER FOUR

EMILY had never imagined such ecstasy existed, and as the rippling aftermath of pleasure receded and her breathing steadied a beauteous smile curved her swollen lips. She savoured the weight of Anton lying over her, the heavy pounding of his heart against hers.

'I am too heavy,' he rasped.

'No, perfect,' she murmured and felt the warmth of Anton's breath against her throat as he rolled off her.

Her blue eyes misty, she watched him walk to the bathroom, and return moments later, his great body bronzed and glistening with beads of perspiration. 'Come back to bed.'

He lay down beside her, supporting himself on one elbow, his dark eyes searching hers. 'Anton.' She lifted a hand to brush the damp fall of hair from his brow. 'I never knew love could be so...' She was lost for words except to say, 'I love you.' She couldn't stop saying it. 'I love everything about you.' Her finger traced the line of his cheekbone, his strong chin shadowed with dark stubble. She sighed. He was so magnificent...so perfect...and incredibly she felt slow-building warmth once again in her slender body.

'Why didn't you tell me you were a virgin?' He shook his head, and her hand slipped to his broad shoulder, relishing the feel of his smooth skin beneath her fingers.

'Does it matter? We are truly married now,' she said, but her smile faded a little as she looked into his eyes. They were no longer gleaming with desire, but narrowed in angry puzzlement on her face.

'But you were engaged to be married once before. How could it be?'

Emily was surprised and intrigued. How did Anton know she had been engaged before? She was sure she had never told him, and without a second thought she asked him.

'Someone must have mentioned it,' he dismissed, and she had the oddest notion he was avoiding a direct answer. 'But that is not important; you should have told me I was your first.'

'Why? Would you have refused to make love to me if I had?' she teased, and stroked a slender finger down his chest. Slowly, sensually…

'Yes… No… But I could have been more careful if I had known.'

She lifted both her hands and ran her fingers through his black hair, holding his head firmly between her palms. Her blue eyes were sparkling with devilment. 'Well, you can be careful the next time.' And pulled his head down, wanting to kiss him.

She heard the husky rumble of his laugh and suddenly he turned, and in one fluid moment he pulled her on top of him. She wriggled a little, her legs parting to enclose his strong thighs, and heard his sharp intake of breath with feminine satisfaction.

'For an innocent I have a feeling you are going to be a very fast study,' he said with husky amusement in his tone.

'I hope so,' she quipped, and ran her hand over the soft curling hairs of his chest, her finger grazing a very male nipple. 'When does the next lesson begin?' she asked mischievously, resting her chin on his breastbone and looking up into his darkly handsome face.

His sensuous grin sent a delicious shiver the length of her spine. 'I think I have awakened a sleeping tigress, and the first thing you need to know is the male takes a little longer to recover than the female, though it is a known fact that with a little encouragement the waiting time can be reduced.'

'Like this, you mean,' she prompted softly, and dipped her head to brush his lips with hers, and then his throat, and finally her tongue slipped out to lick a hard male nipple. She loved the musky male taste of him; she could not get enough of him, revelling in the strong hard body beneath her. She trailed one hand down over his rock-hard diaphragm, her slender fingers tracing the slim line of black body hair down to the flat plane of his belly, and lower to explore his essential maleness, and very quickly the waiting was over.

Time had no meaning as they explored the hunger, the depths of passion and the exquisite tenderness of their love. They bathed and made love again, slept and made love again...

Emily yawned and opened her eyes to find Anton standing over her dressed in khaki shorts and a white polo shirt, and holding a coffee-cup in his hand. Sleepily she looked at him, a slow beautiful smile curving her full lips.

'You're up,' she murmured and her stomach gave a distinct rumble. 'What time is it?'

He grinned and placed the cup and saucer on the bedside table. 'One.' Then he bent his head to drop a swift kiss on her brow.

She frowned. 'It's the middle of the night. Come back to bed.'

'It is one on Thursday afternoon.'

'Oh, hell!' she exclaimed and stretched, then winced as muscles she never knew she had stung. 'I must get up.' She started to, then realized she was naked, and, finding the cotton coverlet, she tugged it over her body.

* * *

Anton winced guiltily with her, his dark eyes roaming over her lithe, shapely form. She looked so delectable, her blonde hair tousled around her beautiful face, her lips pink and swollen from his kisses, and the sheet barely covering her luscious breasts.

He had bedded some of the most stunning women in the world, but none came close to Emily. She was perfection incarnate, and he knew the image of her naked body, the wild passion they had shared, would be for ever etched in his brain. She had been a virgin, and he should have had more control, and he had *tried*.

After the second time, he had carried her to the bathroom and bathed her, but by the time he had got around to drying her he had lost control again, then he had given up counting. He had never known a woman like her in his life; she was all Eve, a temptress, and a siren with a body to drive a man out of his mind.

As he had expected from the first time he laid eyes on Emily, she was a sexy, passionate woman. She had gone up in flames as soon as he touched her. She had wreathed in his arms, and cried his name, cried out her love as he possessed her exquisite body, convulsing in orgasmic pleasure time after time.

What was even more amazing, with remarkable aptitude in no time at all she learnt just what buttons to press to make him equally helpless in the power of their passion. She was a naturally born sensualist...

The only thing he had not expected was that she would still be a virgin. The man she had been engaged to before must have been a eunuch or an absolute saint.

He found it incredible that he was her first lover. He had never made love to a virgin before. Innocence had never appealed to him, he preferred experienced women who knew the score, and yet he was stunned by the uniquely erotic experience. And if he was honest, in a totally chauvinistic way he felt an overwhelming masculine satisfaction and pride that she had given her virginity to him. She was his…only his…

He didn't believe in love, but there was something extremely beguiling in having a wildly sexy wife who did. He had intended revealing the true reason he had married her after spending one passionate night with her. But he had already virtually dismissed the idea on the plane over here, and now, having discovered how innocent she was, he would have to be the biggest fool in Christendom to disillusion her. Anton was no fool and he thanked his lucky stars he had kept his mouth shut about her father.

His body hardened just looking at her and his mouth tightened as he fought the temptation to join her in bed, captivated by her every movement as she reached for the cup he had left for her on the bedside table.

'Good idea, drink your coffee,' he finally answered, 'and join me in the salon when you are dressed.' He didn't trust himself to keep his hands off her, and she needed time to recover. 'The chef has prepared lunch and then I will give you a tour of the yacht and introduce you to the captain and crew.' Turning on his heel, he walked rather stiffly out of the cabin.

Emily drank the coffee and, sliding off the bed, headed for the shower. Washed and wearing only a towel, she glanced around the cabin and saw her suitcase standing by a wall of cupboards. She had never thought of unpacking it the night before. In a matter of minutes she unpacked her trousseau so carefully bought over the last few weeks. One exquisite evening gown, and a host of smart summer clothes, some stylish if slightly risqué lingerie and bikinis courtesy of Helen.

As she closed the lingerie drawer a secret smile curved her

lips at the thought of wearing them for Anton. She slipped on lace briefs and a matching bra, and a pair of white cotton shorts and a blue cotton top she had chosen to wear. She brushed her hair back off her face and fastened it with a slide. She didn't bother with make-up, just a sun screen; she was in a hurry to get back to her husband.

After lunch, Anton spent the next three hours giving Emily a tour of the yacht and introducing her to the captain and crew. The chief steward and the chef, he explained, arranged all the catering and the domestic running of the yacht. She wowed them all with her natural ease and grace, and her obvious interest in the mechanics of the yacht. Surprisingly for a woman she was quite knowledgeable about the workings of a ship.

While he appreciated her interest, after half an hour all he wanted to do was get her back into bed. Her fantastically long legs were displayed in all their glory by the shorts she was wearing and he could not keep his eyes off her. It hadn't escaped his notice neither could any other man around.

'So what do you think, Emily?' he asked as he leant against the ship's rail, and clasped his hands loosely around her waist, and drew her between his splayed legs.

'I think it is the ultimate boys' toy.' She looked up at him with such love and laughter in her eyes, inexplicably his heart tightened and his body followed suit. 'I have seen cruise liners smaller than this.' She shook her head in amazement. 'I am not surprised we are anchored offshore—there is probably not a berth big enough even in Monte Carlo.' She laughed. 'I knew you were wealthy, but I had no idea how rich.' She grinned up at him. 'A helipad, a swimming pool and a wicked-looking motor launch to take us ashore. It is unbelievable, I love it, and I love you.' And he felt the touch of her lips against his chin.

'Then that is all right,' Anton answered gruffly, swallowing a peculiar lump in his throat.

'But what I want to know is when are we sailing and where to? The captain, when I asked him, did not seem to know. Is our honeymoon going to be a mystery tour?' she demanded with a chuckle, and moved seductively between his thighs increasing the ever-present sensual awareness between them.

Her bare legs brushing his sent his temperature soaring and Anton hardened still further; he could not help himself. But her question reminded him of where they were and why, and he felt a bit selfish, not a feeling he was comfortable with. He tightened his hands on her waist and lightly urged her back, then dropped his hands from her far-too-tempting body.

He let his gaze rest on her lovely face; her luminous eyes revealed her every thought. She was so open, so affectionate and this was her honeymoon.

His black brows pleated in a frown as belatedly he realized his decision to use the long-standing arrangement he had made for his annual trip to the Formula One Monaco Grand Prix to double as a honeymoon no longer seemed quite so reasonable. Emily had probably been expecting a romantic out-of-the-way place and just the two of them. Whereas he, without a second thought given the reason he had married her, had decided to do what he always did at this time of year, confident that Emily would fit in with his plans.

His frown deepened. He had never had to consider a woman's feelings before. Every woman he had known in the past had been quite happy to pander to his every whim, and why not? He was an extremely wealthy man and a generous lover for as long as an affair lasted. He had made it clear from the outset he never had any intention of marrying them, all he had wanted was good sex. He didn't do romance, and he wasn't about to start now simply because he was married.

Married to the daughter of the man who destroyed his sister, he reminded himself. He had been in danger of forgetting that fact in the throes of what was basically nothing more than great sex, he reasoned. Straightening his broad shoulders, he told her the truth.

'There is no mystery; I stay here at the end of May every year for the motor racing. The Monaco Grand Prix is on Sunday. As a sponsor for one of the teams, I usually watch the race from the pits. Then there is an after-race party,' he explained, studying her reaction through narrowed eyes.

'Oh, I see.' Her blue eyes shaded and Anton knew she did not see at all. 'I never realized you were a racing-car enthusiast, though I suppose I should have guessed. Boys' toys again, hmm? Well, it will be another new experience, I suppose.' And her sensuous lips curled in a bewitching smile. 'At least I will have you to myself until Sunday.'

Frustration and the fact she was so damn reasonable angered Anton. That and the unfamiliar feeling of guilt that assailed him because he had not told her the half of it yet. For a brief moment he wondered if he could just order the captain to set sail immediately, but dismissed the notion.

Emily was his wife, his extraordinarily beautiful, incredible, sexy wife, but he changed his plans for no one, and he wasn't about to start now. He had his life organized exactly as he liked it, and although Emily had a career it was pretty flexible—she would quickly adjust and go where he led.

'Not exactly…' He paused. 'I don't use the yacht solely for my own pleasure; sometimes it is chartered out. It would not be financially viable otherwise. But also as a single man up until now,' he swiftly added, 'it has been a convenient way to repay hospitality rather than the more conventional house party.' He was prevaricating…not like him at all, and bluntly he told her, 'Anyway, it has become a bit of a tradition of mine to invite a few like-minded guests whose hospitality I have enjoyed in the past to join me on board for the Grand Prix weekend, and they usually stay until Monday.'

For a long moment Emily simply stared at her very new husband. He was standing, his long body taut, apparently unconcerned. But she caught a glimmer of uncertainty in the depths of his dark eyes, probably a first for him, and she hid a smile. Anton had it all. Wealth, power, and as a one-hundred-per-cent-virile male he was accustomed to doing exactly what he wanted to do without ever having to consider anyone else. Women had been falling over themselves to please him all his adult life, if rumours were to be believed. But he obviously had a lot to learn about marriage—they both did.

'Let me get this straight—you have invited guests on our honeymoon to watch motor racing. Yes?'

'Yes,' he said with a negligent shrug of his broad shoulder.

'A novel honeymoon.' Emily placed a slender hand on his chest. 'But, hey, I am all for tradition, and if this is a tradition of yours, why not? In fact it will be nice to meet some of your friends. So far I have only met business acquaintances—and Max, of course. He made a very good best man, and where is he, by the way?' she asked. 'He came on board with us last night.'

'He has gone ashore in the launch,' he said, avoiding her eyes. 'The guests are arriving this evening.'

Anton was obviously embarrassed, Emily thought, and, while she wasn't delighted at the idea of spending the weekend with strangers, she allowed her smile to break free.

'Don't look so serious, Anton. It's okay. We have only known each other a couple of months, but we have a lifetime together to get on the same wavelength.' Standing on tiptoe, she kissed his cheek.

'My mum told me she and my dad fell in love at first sight. They got engaged after four months and married two months after that. They had only ever lived with their parents until they married and it took time to adjust, especially as they were both virgins when they met. At least I have started off with a great lover even if you are dumb when it comes to arranging a honeymoon.'

Anton's eyes narrowed incredulously on her smiling face and he was not in the least amused, the mention of her father hitting a raw nerve.

'Dumb,' he repeated. She had the cheek to call him dumb. Was she for real?

He scowled down at her and noted the shimmering sensuality in her sparkling eyes, and he did not know if he wanted to shake her or kiss her... For a man who prided himself on his control, he did not like the ambivalent way she made him feel. She looked about seventeen dressed in white shorts and a blue tee shirt the colour of her eyes, and her hair pulled back in a slide, and her youthful appearance simply increased his unwelcome sense of guilt and anger.

'For God's sake, Emily, you are the only dumb one around here. You can't possibly believe that rubbish you are spouting. Your mother might have been a virgin, but your father certainly wasn't. Trust me, I know,' he declared with biting cynicism.

Emily's euphoric mood took a huge knock. She stumbled back a step, her blue eyes widening at the icy expression on his brutally handsome face. The lover of a few hours ago had gone and in his place was the man with the cold, remote eyes that she had seen on the night they first met.

'You knew my father?' she asked, feeling her way through

an atmosphere that was suddenly fraught with tension. 'You met him?'

'No, I never met him, but I didn't need to to know what a womanizer he was.'

Emily could not let his slur on her father pass.

'As you never met my father you can't possibly know that. But I do know that my mother never lied,' she argued in defence of her parents. She loved Anton, she had married him, but she was not going to let him walk all over her. It was bad enough she was going to share the first few days of her honeymoon with a group of strangers. 'You're not infallible, you know, and in this case you are wrong.'

Anton heard the belligerence in her voice, saw the defiance in her glittering blue eyes and was outraged that she was daring to argue with him. Very few people argued with him and nobody doubted his word. He could not quite believe his very new wife had the nerve to say he was wrong.

'Your mother must have been as naive as you,' he opined scathingly, 'if she believed Charles Fairfax was anything other than a womanizing swine and a snob to boot.' He was seething with anger and it made him say more than he intended. 'He probably only married her for her aristocratic connection.'

Without her giving it a second thought Emily's hand scythed through the air, but Anton's strong hand caught her wrist before she could make contact with his arrogant face.

'You little hellcat.' He twisted her hand behind her back and hauled her hard against his long body. 'You dare to lash out at me, because I have told you a few home truths about your sainted family.'

'At least I have one,' Emily spat, and was immediately disgusted with herself for what was a low blow. But somehow the passion Anton aroused in her sexually seemed to just as easily arouse her anger. She who was normally the most placid of women, and it shocked her.

She glanced up at him. He was looking at her with eyes as cold as the Arctic waste. Then abruptly he let go of her wrist and moved back as though he could not bear to touch her.

'And do you know why I have not, Emily?' he said with a sardonic arch of one black brow, and, not waiting for her to answer, he added, 'Because of your lech of a father.'

'You never knew my father, and yet you seem to dislike him,' she murmured. She knew it from the animosity in his tone, the tension in his body, and suddenly she was afraid.

His handsome face hardened. 'Dislike is too tame a word. I hate and despise the man, and I have every right to.'

Emily shook her head, trying to make sense of what was happening. She was too shocked to speak. How had they gone from a simmering sensual awareness to a senseless argument in minutes?

'Once I had an older sister, Suki, a beautiful gentle girl. She was eighteen, barely more than a child herself, when she met Charles Fairfax. He seduced her and left her pregnant with his child. Five months later, after learning Fairfax had married your mother, she committed suicide. Obviously he was seeing both of them at the same time.'

All the colour leached from Emily's face. This was no senseless argument, but deadly serious. She had never even known Anton had a sister. But there was no mistaking the absolute conviction in Anton's voice, and for him to have apparently held a grudge against her father for over a quarter of a century she found totally appalling. She could not believe what she was hearing, didn't want to.

'No, that cannot be true.' She murmured a denial. 'My father would never have betrayed my mother.'

'Believe me, it is,' he said harshly. 'Women who foolishly imagine they are in love are dangerous to themselves as well as to others. My mother never fully recovered from the loss of her daughter and I was kept in ignorance of the full facts for decades. As a boy of eleven I was told Suki had died in a tragic car accident. It was only when my mother was dying I discovered the real truth.'

Her blue eyes widened in horror as she recognized the latent anger in his black eyes, the brooding expression on his face, and knew he totally believed what he had just told her. And with the knowledge came pain, a pain that built and built as the full import of his words sank into her brain.

'When did your mother die?'

He frowned down at her. 'Does it matter? Last December.'

Oh, my God! Only six months ago. No wonder Anton was so angry, with the death of his mother, the pain of losing his sister must have hit him all over again. From that thought came another, deeply disturbing. Shortly after his mother's death Anton had made the acquaintance of her brother and uncle, and taken an interest in the Fairfax family and then in her. Coincidence—or something much worse, and a cold dread enveloped her.

Her eyes swept helplessly over him, the bold attractive face, the strong tanned throat revealed by the open neck of his polo shirt, the khaki shorts that hugged his lean hips ending mid-thigh and his long legs. Her heart squeezed as vivid images of his naked body flashed in her mind, the body she had worshipped last night. Anton, the man she loved, and had been certain loved her. But not any more...

CHAPTER FIVE

ANTON had shaken her world on its axis and Emily was no longer certain of anything. She could not bear to look at him.

Her mind spinning, she let her gaze roam over the view of the tiny principality. The sea as smooth as glass, the spectacular marina, the gleaming buildings were picture-postcard perfect, but wasted on her. She needed to think…

The sun was still shining but the warmth no longer seemed to touch her. Yesterday she had been a blushing bride confident in the love of her husband, but now… She let her mind wander back over the first time they had met, the sequence of events, the conversations, his proposal of marriage that had led to this moment, and belatedly she realized he had never actually said he loved her…

Not even last night in the heat of passion had the word love passed his lips.

Emily shivered as cold fingers seemed to grip her heart, the icy tendrils spreading slowly through every part of her. She was an intelligent woman, and suddenly her whirlwind courtship and fairy-tale marriage were falling apart before her eyes. Slowly she turned her head and allowed her gaze to rest on her husband's hard, expressionless face.

'Why did you marry me, Anton?'

'I decided it was time I took a wife and produced an heir. I chose you because I thought you were a beautiful, sensuous woman who would fit me perfectly.' He reached out a hand to her. 'And I was right,' he stated.

Emily batted his hand away. 'And the rest.' She stared up at him ashen-faced, horrified at the cynical practicality of his reasoning, but instinctively knowing there was more he was not telling her.

'I might be dumb. But I am not that dumb. You only came into contact with my family after the death of your mother, and I don't believe in coincidences. You might as well tell me the whole truth.' And, though her heart was shattering into a million pieces, bravely she added, 'Because it is becoming increasingly obvious you did not marry me for love.' She prayed he would contradict her, declare he loved her and it was all a horrible mistake.

'Why not?' Anton said with a shrug of his broad shoulders. 'You are now my wife—Mrs Emily Diaz, a name your father refused to acknowledge or be associated with, and it satisfies my sense of justice to know you have my name for the rest of your life.'

His dark eyes, a gleam of mocking triumph in their inky depths, clashed with her pained blue. 'As for love, I don't believe in it myself. Though women seem to have a desperate need to. What we shared last night and will continue to share is great sexual chemistry, not love.'

Tears blurred Emily's vision and fiercely she blinked them away. So this was what it felt like to crash and burn. All her hopes and dreams ground to dust in a few short minutes. For a short while, a very brief two months, Anton had been the man she loved. For an even briefer twenty-four hours she had been his wife. He had made love to her, and it had been the most amazing experience of her life and she had thought she was the luckiest woman in the world to be loved by him.

But it had not been love… He freely admitted it was simply sex, nothing more.

For Anton yesterday had been about sex and some misguided notion of retribution, not love, never love…

How could she have been such a blind idiot? She had known the first time she set eyes on him, he was dangerous. She had avoided going out with him for a week. She should have trusted her gut instinct about the man.

Her shimmering blue eyes swept over him, noted the arrogant certainty in his gaze. The Anton he had been when they had first got together, the man she had thought had refrained from making love to her because he respected her, bore no relationship to the Anton before her now. Cold and cynical, he was not the man she had fallen in love with.

She shook her head in disgust, nausea clawing at her stomach as she was forced to accept the man she thought she loved did not exist… 'I need the bathroom.'

'Wait.' He grasped her upper arm, halting her retreat. 'This does not change anything, Emily.'

'It does for me.' She looked at him. 'Let me go.' And she meant it in every sense of the word. 'I really do need the bathroom.'

Anton's mouth twisted. 'Of course.' He removed his hand from her arm, wondering why the hell he had told Emily about her father when not long ago he had been thanking his lucky stars he had kept his mouth shut.

But then from the minute he had watched her walk down the aisle he had not been his rational self. The woman had that effect on him. Last night he had lost control in bed, a first for him, and this afternoon he had lost his temper at the mention of her father. He was going weak in the head and it had to stop.

Honesty was supposed to be good for a marriage; he'd been honest, he reasoned arrogantly. It was Emily who was unreasonable.

'Arguing on the deck is not a great idea. We can talk later. After all, neither of us is going anywhere,' he said dismissively.

He would catch up on some work—he had let things slide a little in his pursuit of Emily and it would give her time to cool down. She said she loved him, and she certainly wanted him. Given his experience of her sex, she'd soon get over the shock of realizing her father had feet of clay after a few days in his bed.

Emily heard the threat in his words and glanced at him in disgust and walked away. Was he really so cold, so insensitive to believe for a second they could carry on as husband and wife now she knew why he had really married her?

Emily walked into the cabin and locked the door behind her. Blindly she headed for the bathroom, and was violently sick. She began to shake uncontrollably and, ripping off her clothes, she stepped into the shower. She turned the water on full, and only then did she give way to the tears. She cried until she could cry no more. Then slowly she straightened and, picking up the shampoo provided, she washed her hair, and then scrubbed every inch of her body, trying to scrub away the scent, the memory of Anton's touch from every pore of her skin. Trying to scrub away the pain, she had a hollow feeling that would be with her for the rest of her life…

She did not know the man she had married, had never known him. It was Nigel all over again, but worse, because she had been foolish enough to marry Anton. Nigel had wanted her for her supposed fortune and connections, and Anton—he had married her simply because her name was Fairfax. He had seduced her into marriage because he believed her father had seduced his sister. To fulfil a primitive need for revenge…no more or less…and she could not pretend otherwise.

The pain, the sense of betrayal were excruciating, but slowly as she finished washing, turned off the shower and wrapped a large towel around her naked body the pain was overtaken by a cold, numbing anger.

She thought of her parents, and, no matter what the arrogant Anton Diaz thought, she knew her father was incapable of doing what he had said. Her parents had loved each other, they had married in their twenties, and when her mother had died it had broken her father's heart. She firmly believed it was the stress of losing his wife that had helped cause the heart attack that had killed him far too young.

It was her mother who, when she was terminally ill, had constantly told Emily to embrace life to the full, and not to waste time dwelling on past failures or grudges—life was much too short. A theory her uncle Clive had first taught her when as a child of twelve she had had to accept she was never going to be a ballet dancer.

A trait that Emily had inherited from the Deveral side of her family.

So why was she even giving Anton's tragic tale a second thought? Where he had got it from she had no idea, and she cared even less. As for her marriage, as far as she was concerned it was over…

Five minutes later, dressed in casual drawstring linen trousers and a matching sleeveless top, Emily lifted her suitcase onto the bed and began to methodically pack the clothes she had unpacked only hours before.

She heard a knock on the door but ignored it.

She was immune to everything except the need to leave. She snapped the suitcase shut, and straightened up. Now all she needed was her travel bag and she was out of here.

'Just what the hell do you think you are doing?' a deep voice roared. And Emily spun round to see Anton striding towards her. 'How dare you lock me out?' he demanded. His black eyes leaping with fury, he grasped her shoulder. 'What the hell do you think you are playing at, woman?'

'I am not playing. I am leaving… The game is over,' she said, standing tall and proud. 'Your game,' she said bitterly.

Emily felt nothing for him. She was cocooned in a block of ice. The hands on her shoulders, the close proximity of his big body had no effect on her. Except to reinforce her determination to leave. It was bad enough she had made the mistake of marrying him. She was certainly not going to allow him to manhandle her.

Anton was furious. He had got no work done, he couldn't seem to concentrate, and finally he had given up and decided to smooth things over with Emily, only to find she had locked him out of their cabin. Not that it mattered—he had a master-key. But his temper was at breaking-point.

'Over my dead body.'

'That would be my preference,' Emily tossed back.

She felt his great body tense and his hands fell from her shoulders. She watched his handsome face darken and for a second she thought she saw a flash of pain in his eyes, and for a moment she was ashamed of her hateful comment. She would not wish anybody dead. But Anton had the knack of making her say and feel things she did not want to.

'Well, I think I can safely say, barring accidents, you will not get your wish any time soon. Though for the foreseeable future it appears I must watch my back where you are concerned, my sweet loving wife, because I have no intention of letting you leave. Not now. Not ever.'

'You have no choice.' She tilted up her chin and drew on

every ounce of her pride to face him. 'As far as I am concerned the marriage is finished.'

Anton's dark eyes studied her.

He was furious at her defiance but he did not let it show. Because in a way he could understand her distress, her desire to lash back at him, though he had not appreciated her wishing him dead.

He didn't do emotions, other than over death and birth maybe. But Emily was an emotional, passionate woman, as she had proved spectacularly last night. She had been brought up on love and happy ever after. Hell, he could still hear her cries of love ringing in his ears when he had taken possession of her exquisite body. And he would again, he thought confidently. She just needed time to adjust to the reality of life as his wife.

'We always have a choice, Emily,' he murmured silkily, and, snaking an arm around her waist, he pulled her into the strength of his powerful body. 'Your choice is quite simple. You stay with me, your *husband*,' he emphasized, grasping her chin between his fingers and tilting her face up to his. 'You behave civilly as my wife and the perfect hostess I know you to be with our guests and you can continue to dabble at your career until you're pregnant with my child. Something that was implicit in the promise you made yesterday, I seem to recall.'

She stared at him. 'That was before I knew the truth. Now let me go.'

Her usual luminous blue eyes were impenetrable, her body rigid in his hold, and it made Anton want to pierce her icy control... Something he would never have imagined she was capable of.

'You have two choices. One, you stay with me. The other is you return to your brother's home, and his pregnant wife, and inform them you have left me.' He let his hand stroke down her throat, a finger resting on the pulse that beat wildly in her neck. Not such icy control as he had thought…

'Then you can explain that naturally, as I am deeply upset, I am severing all ties with your family,' he drawled with mocking sarcasm. 'Which unfortunately for Fairfax Engineering will mean an immediate repayment of the loans I forwarded some months ago for the expansion of the company.'

Then, like all good predators, he watched and waited for his victim to recognize her fate.

He saw the puzzled expression on her face, could almost see her mind assimilating what he had said, and knew the moment she realized. Anger flared in her wide blue eyes and flags of colour stained her cheeks. She twisted out of his hold and he let her, smiling inwardly. He knew she was not going anywhere…

Emily took a few steps back on legs that trembled. The numbness that had protected her since his shocking revelation about her father was fading fast and the effort to remain un-affected by his closeness had taken every bit of control she possessed. She was horribly conscious that just being held against him had made her traitorous body aching‑y aware of him and was furious at herself and him… She drew in a few deep steadying breaths and wrapped her arms defensively around her midriff, grittily determined to control her anger and the rest…

The silence lengthened.

She could feel Anton watching, waiting, and finally, when she was confident she could speak to him without tearing the lying rat's eyes out, she glanced across at him.

'And what exactly does that mean for Fairfax?' she asked in a cool little voice.

'An educated guess. The expansion will have to stop and they will be in deep financial trouble, and probably ripe for a hostile takeover.' He gave her a humourless smile. 'As I said before, the choice is yours, Emily.'

He didn't need to add a takeover by him. Emily figured that out for herself. 'You would do that...' she prompted, and saw his proud head incline slightly, the glimmer of triumph in his dark eyes, and she knew the answer.

'If I have to. I will do anything to keep you.'

A hysterical laugh rose in her throat and she choked it back. *He would do anything to keep her.* A few hours ago she would have been flattered by his words, now she was just sickened.

Suddenly her legs threatened to collapse beneath her, and abruptly she sat down on the bed, her hands clasped tightly in her lap, and stared up at him in sheer disbelief...

She shook her head and looked down at her hands, her gaze lingering on the gold band on her finger. What a travesty...

Slowly she reran the scenario of the future of their marriage Anton had painted in her head. It did not take a genius to work out he must have planned this all along. She also realized there was one glaring flaw in the choice he had given her as far as she was concerned.

'If what you say is true you can take the company any time, whether we are together or not,' she said slowly. 'And you freely admit you don't love me, or anyone else for that matter. We both know you can have any woman you want without much effort, and frequently do by all accounts.' Though picturing him in another woman's arms doing what he had done to her was like a knife to her heart. She paused for a moment, drawing on every bit of will-power she could before lifting her head and asking, 'So why on earth, Anton, would I stay with you?'

He stood towering over her, his expression unreadable. He was so close she imagined she felt the warmth of his body reaching out to her, and she trembled and despised herself for it.

Then he smiled—he actually smiled, all confident macho male, and she wanted to thump him. He sat down beside her, his great body angled towards her, and hastily she moved away, but banged against her damn suitcase and sent it tumbling to the floor.

'Steady, Emily.' He reached across her to put a restraining hand on her arm and she flinched at the contact. 'And though I am flattered you think I can have any woman I want, I want only you.'

Anton knew he had her. He had noted her tremble. His original assessment was right—in a few days she would forget this nonsense about leaving him. But he had to tread warily. Naturally she was upset and angry because he had forced her to face reality and accept he was not quite the Prince Charming she had imagined…but as human as the next man.

He had not got where he was today without being ruthless when it came to what he wanted. He never took an insult to his integrity without seeking retribution. Anything less was a sign of weakness, and no one could accuse him of that.

But he could do charming…

She was as skittish as the newborn foals he bred on his ranch in Peru and needed gentle handling. She would stay with him anyway, of that he was determined. But he would prefer her to stay with him willingly and what he wanted he always got.

'I regret arguing with you, but you have a knack of inflaming all my passions.' He grimaced. 'I never meant to tell you the truth about your father, but your rosy view of him spiked my temper and for that I apologize. So now can we put this argument behind us, and get on with our marriage? It is up to you, Emily, but I promise if you stay I will never harm your family firm in any way.' He reached for her hand, and he found he was grasping air as she shot off the bed at the speed of light, and spun around to stare down at him.

Surprise didn't cut it; he had been at his caring best, what more did she want? His mouth grim, Anton studied her. God, she was magnificent. Statuesque, her blue eyes blazing, her perfect breasts rising and falling in her agitation, her hands placed defiantly on her slender hips. He was aroused simply looking at her, and then she spoke, and his softly-softly approach flew out of the window.

'Are you mad? After today I would not believe a word you said if you swore it on a stack of bibles,' she yelled.

'Then trust this,' Anton snarled, his temper and frustration finally boiling over, and, catching her around the waist, he tumbled her onto the bed.

The breath left Emily's body and before she knew it she was flat on her back with Anton's long body pinning her to the bed.

For a moment she was too shocked to move, and then his mouth was crashing down on hers, and instantly her pulse rate surged and she was wildly, passionately angry. She fought like a woman possessed, she kicked out and he retaliated by pinning her legs between his heavy thighs. She bit his tongue, her hands tangled in his hair and pulled. He did the same.

'Hell—Emily—'

His voice was ragged and then his mouth slammed back down on hers. Still she tried to resist, but his big body pressed against her, his hand in her hair holding her firm, his other hand cupping her breast, kneading, igniting a different kind of passion.

His hand left her hair, and he shoved her top and bra up over her breasts, his mouth covering her already-straining nipples. Wild excitement ripped through her and all thought of resistance was blown away in the storm of passion engulfing her.

'You want me,' he rasped.

'Yes,' she groaned, her arms involuntarily wrapping around him. She didn't notice when he removed her trousers. She wanted him; he was right—she could not help herself.

His lips brushed her breast, her throat, her mouth, and her mouth twined with his in a desperate greedy kiss. Involuntarily her slender body arched up beneath him, and she gloried in the pressure of his surging masculine arousal. He moved sensually against her, and she moaned as his teeth and tongue found her aching nipples, teasing and tasting until she was wild with wanting. Anton's hands curved around her buttocks and her body jerked violently as he plunged to the hilt into the sleek, tight centre of her, the sensation so intense, she could barely breathe.

Hard and fast, he thrust repeatedly, and her body convulsed in an explosion of pleasure so exquisite she could only gasp as he plunged on to his own shuddering release.

She lay there, her eyes closed, exhausted and fighting for breath, the shuddering aftermath still pulsing inside her. She felt Anton roll off her and say her name. But she kept her eyes closed. She could not face him, a deep sense of shame and humiliation consuming her.

Knowing he did not love her and had an ulterior motive for marrying her... Nothing had stopped her melting like ice in the sun as soon as he had kissed her. In one passionate encounter he had turned her lifelong belief in love on its head. She felt his hand smoothing back her hair from her face, his fingers trace the curve of her mouth.

'Emily, look at me.'

Reluctantly she opened her eyes. He was leaning over her, determination in every angle of his brutally handsome face.

'No more pretence, Emily. You want me and I want you. You may already be carrying my child, so no more arguments. We are married and that is the way it is going to stay.'

She almost told him then...

Emily was a practical woman and she had started taking the pill a week after their first date as a precaution for the affair she had hoped would follow, marriage not on her mind at the time. Now she kept her secret. Why feed his colossal ego by letting him know how ridiculously eager she had been to go to bed with him?

'And I have no say in the matter.'

'No.' Anton's dark eyes swept over her, his lips curving in a brief satisfied smile as he straightened up, flexing his shoulders. 'Your body said it for you.'

He was so damned arrogant, Emily thought bitterly. He was standing at the foot of the bed, his shirt in place and zipping his shorts, and suddenly a fiery tide of red washed over her as she realized he had not even removed his clothing. Whereas she… She looked down… Oh, God… Hastily she tugged her bra and top down over her breasts. She was mortified and glanced wildly around for her trousers.

'Yours, I believe,' Anton drawled, a hint of amusement in his black eyes as he dropped her white trousers and briefs on her legs. 'Though you might like to change for dinner—our guests will be arriving soon.' And he strolled out of the cabin without a backward glance, while Emily fumed.

She leapt off the bed, and headed straight for the shower for the third time that day. She wasted no time, knowing Anton would be back to change.

Washed and wearing only bra and briefs, she unpacked her case yet again. She would allow Anton to think she agreed with him, until she could figure out a way to leave without harming her family.

She chose a short, black, thankfully crease-proof slip dress, and put it on. She slapped some moisturizer on her face, covered her lips in pink gloss and brushed her hair. She saw no reason in dressing up to the nines for Anton and his friends. They were not hers and never would be now. He had had the nerve to say earlier she could dabble with her career until the children arrived. The word 'dabble' said it all. So much for his promise to support her given on the night he proposed. He obviously had no respect for who or what she was. As for children... She hardened her heart against the image of a dark-haired beautiful baby, a replica of Anton, in her arms... Like all her foolish dreams of love, that was never going to happen now.

She slid her feet into black sandals, and exited the cabin. She needed some fresh air.

Emily walked to the seaward side of the yacht and, half hidden by a lifeboat, she leant against the rail to watch the thin crescent of the sun sink beneath the horizon in a last red blaze of glory. She stood for a long time, her mind swirling, trying to find a way out. She looked at the darkening night sky and felt as though the same darkness were wrapping its way around her heart and soul.

She would never do anything that might harm her brother and family. After today, her trust in Anton was totally shattered. How could she love a man she didn't trust? It wasn't possible. Yet when he had tumbled her on the bed her anger had been fierce but fleeting, she had welcomed his possession, and with bitter self-loathing she knew she would again. She was helpless to resist. She also knew she had no alternative but to go along with what he wanted. She was trapped...

CHAPTER SIX

EMILY heard the sound of raised voices and realized the launch must have arrived with the guests, but she didn't move, reluctant to go and face strangers with her emotions so raw.

A deep painful sigh escaped her. Short of discovering she had married a homicidal maniac, she must have had the worst first day of marriage in history. Still, it couldn't possibly get any worse, she told herself, and, taking a deep breath, she turned.

'Emily.' Anton was moving towards her. He was dressed in a lightweight beige suit, his shirt open at the neck, and his black hair slicked severely back from his brow, and she realized with a sick sense of shame he looked more gorgeous than ever to her tortured mind.

'I wondered where you were hiding,' he drawled sardonically. 'Our guests have arrived.' He took her arm and led her into the salon.

Emily was wrong: the day could get worse…

Seated on Anton's left, Emily glanced around the table. The dinner party from hell was a pretty fair assessment, she mused.

They were seven couples in all, a single young man and, with the inclusion of Max, sixteen around the dinner table in the sumptuous dining area of the yacht.

Anton at his eloquent best had introduced her as his wife, and she would have to have been an idiot not to notice the surprise and outright disbelief at his pronouncement. While in an aside to her he had warned her to behave impeccably in front of his guests…or else…

Else what? Emily wondered. He could not hurt her any more than he already had. The congratulations were gushing, but the looks she got from the six other women on board varied from genuine pleasure to curiosity to almost pitying and, from one, simply venomous.

She smiled and Anton kept the conversation going with very little help from her through five courses that she barely remembered eating. She was in shock.

Wouldn't you just know it? she mused. The first person she had seen was Eloise. Anton had introduced her to Eloise's Italian husband, Carlo Alviano, and his twenty-two-year-old son from a previous marriage, Gianni.

She raised her glass and took another sip of wine, and glanced around the table. Sally and Tim Harding she recognized from a business dinner she had attended in London with Anton. As for the other four couples, they seemed pleasant enough. One couple was Swiss, another French, and a rather nice middle-aged American couple, and the last pair were Greek. It was a truly international gathering of the seriously rich, and, from the designer dresses and jewellery on show, she wouldn't like to estimate how much their combined worth came to. Billions no doubt…

She glanced at the young man, Gianni, seated on her right. There was something familiar about him but she could not quite place him. She took another sip of wine, and let her gaze roam over him. He was classically handsome with perfect features and thick black curly hair. Maybe he was a model; perhaps she had seen a picture of him in a magazine.

'More wine?' the steward offered and Emily nodded. She knew she was probably drinking too much, but she was past caring and let her eyes stray to rest on Eloise, with a kind of morbid fascination.

Eloise was obviously Anton's type of woman.

She was wearing a red minidress, that barely covered her voluptuous breasts or her bum. She was seated on the right of Anton and had spent most of the meal trying to hold his attention, gossiping away to him about old times with much touching of his arm and anywhere else she could reach. As for her husband, Carlo, who was seated next to her, she virtually ignored him.

Why Carlo put up with her Emily could not fathom. A sophisticated, handsome man in his fifties, he was quite charming and owned a merchant bank. Maybe that was why Eloise had married him, she thought cynically.

She took another sip of her wine. And maybe Carlo didn't care so long as the sex was good... Maybe he was the same type of man as Anton—look at the reality of her marriage after one day—and she giggled, seeing the black humour in the situation.

'Oh, please, you must share the joke,' Eloise trilled, all fake smiles.

Emily glanced across at her, saw the spite in the other woman's eyes and said, 'It was nothing. Just a humorous thought.'

'Let us be the judge of that,' Eloise prompted. And for one moment Emily was tempted to tell her exactly what she had been thinking. But although she had consumed a little too much wine, it was far from enough for her to make a fool of herself.

'No,' she said and froze into immobility as Anton lifted a hand to her cheek and trailed his fingers down and around the nape of her neck, urging her head towards him.

'Some coffee or water maybe.' His gaze locked with hers and something moved in the dark depths of his eyes. 'You have had a couple of very full days, my darling, as I know,' he drawled, his finger pressing on the pulse that beat strongly in her throat.

Her eyes widened, and she barely controlled an involuntary shiver until he added, 'Any more wine and you will fall asleep.' And she realized that his show of affection was purely for the guests and to add insult to injury he had implied she was drunk…the swine.

She drew in a deep steadying breath. 'You're right as always, darling,' she mocked, and reached up to remove his hand from her neck, digging her nails into his wrist in the process. 'Coffee, thanks.'

Anton's eyes narrowed, promising retaliation, then he turned to beckon the steward and coffee was provided.

Hot and angry, Emily silently seethed. The atmosphere stank, there was no other word for it, and she wished she could go out on deck for some clean air. Better still dive overboard and swim to shore—it couldn't be more than half a mile…

'That's it,' she cried and slapped her hand on the table, making the glass and cutlery rattle.

'Gianni, I thought I knew you.' She turned to the young man at her side, the first genuine smile of the evening lighting her face. It had come to her out of the blue when she had thought of swimming.

'You were in the under-twenty-ones swimming team for Rome University at the European Universities' sports challenge held in Holland four years ago.'

'Yes, señora, I recognized you immediately, but I thought you did not remember me.'

'Oh, please call me Emily—you did before,' she reminded him. 'I watched you win in an amazing split-second finish in the fifteen hundred metres—you were fantastic, and we met at the party afterwards.'

'That's right, and I saw you win the two hundred metres with two seconds to spare. You were brilliant.'

'Thank you. That was one of my finer moments.' She preened and laughed and so did Gianni.

His father intervened. 'You two know each other.' And his handsome face was wreathed in smiles. 'What a happy coincidence.'

'Yes. And you must be very proud of your son. Did you see him win that race? It was such a close finish after such a long race. He was incredible,' Emily enthused.

'Regrettably, no. I was in South America at the time,' and Emily noticed his eyes stray to Eloise.

'Enough about swimming,' Eloise cut in. 'That is all the boy ever talks about, that and the bank, just like Carlo,' she said petulantly. 'It is so boring.'

'I found it rather enlightening,' Anton said. 'I never knew you were a champion swimmer, Emily.'

Emily caught the faintly sarcastic tone and a hint of anger in the dark eyes that met hers. 'Why should you?' She shrugged. 'You have only known me a couple of months, and anyway I am not any more.'

Suddenly she felt bone-tired. Only an idiot could be unaware of the undercurrent of tension beneath the surface of the supposedly friendly conversation all evening, and it had given her a horrendous headache. That and the appalling realization that all she had to look forward to were countless more such encounters with Anton and his friends had stretched her nerves to breaking-point.

Pushing back her chair, she stood up. 'Well, it has been a delightful evening meeting you all.' She cast a social smile around the table. 'But I am afraid I will have to call it a night. Please excuse me.' The men made to rise. 'No, please, Anton will keep you entertained.'

Anton placed an arm along the back of Emily's waist and she stiffened in shock—she had not realized he had risen with her.

'I will escort you to the cabin, Emily.' His tone was as smooth as silk, and then, raising his voice, he added for his guests' benefit. 'If you need anything ask the steward. I'll be back soon.'

'A champion swimmer. I'm impressed,' Anton declared as he stopped and opened their cabin door, and ushered her inside. 'You are full of surprises, Emily, but if there are any more on the horizon pass them by me first,' he drawled sardonically. 'I do not appreciate being made to look a fool in front of our guests, while you flirt and reminisce with another man.'

'You made to look a fool?' She shook her head and twisted out of his arm to cast him a look of utter disgust. 'I am the only fool around here, for being stupid enough to think I could ever love a man like you. A man who invites his mistress Eloise on his honeymoon.'

'Eloise is not—'

'Oh, please, you have had sex with her; it is in her eyes every time she looks at you. So don't bother denying it.'

'Once, a decade ago,' he snapped. 'Carlo is an old and valued friend of mine and I introduced them. I was best man at their wedding four years ago. Eloise is an old friend, nothing more.'

'You don't need to explain. I couldn't care less, though I am amazed her husband puts up with it—he seems like a really nice man. Whereas you have to be the most devious, arrogant snake of a man it has ever been my misfortune to meet. And if you imagine for one second making me stay with you will change how I think of you...it won't. Now go back to your guests, Anton. I have a headache and I am going to bed. Alone.'

Anton fought down the furious impulse to shut her smart

mouth with his own. 'Not alone, Emily,' he said with implacable softness and took her arm.

She struggled to break free, but he tightened his grip. 'You are my wife and sharing my bed—that is not negotiable.'

His dark brooding eyes held hers. He saw the anger, the pain she tried to hide in the blue depths, and surely not fear?

Shocked, he let go of her arm. He was a huge success at everything he did; women looked at him admiringly, hungrily, with adoration, wanting to please him, but never with fear. So how the hell had he managed to make his bride of one day actually look afraid of him?

'You look worn out. I'll get you some painkillers, and you can get some sleep.'

Hmm. Emily sighed her pleasure as a strong hand slowly massaged her breast. She settled back against a hard male body and arched her neck as firm lips caressed the slender length of her throat, a warm tongue lingering on the steadily beating pulse there. Her eyes half opened and fluttered closed as she gave herself up to the wondrous world of sensations engulfing her. Long fingers caressing, arousing her eager flesh, she was lost in a sensual dream, her heart beating with ever-increasing speed. She turned, restless heat spreading through every cell in her body, her hands curving over strong shoulders. His mouth was on hers, his muscular legs parting hers.

Her eyes flew open. It was no dream—it was Anton lying over her, the morning sun highlighting his blue-black hair, his dark molten eyes scorching through to her soul promising paradise and it was way too late to resist. She didn't want to resist. She wanted him, burned for him. She felt the velvet tip of him against her and raised her pelvis, pressing up to him.

'You want me?' Anton husked throatily.

'Yes, oh, yes,' she moaned.

His hands curved around her thighs, lifting her, and in a single powerful thrust he filled her. He thrust again harder and faster as her body caught his rhythm and they rode a tidal wave of sheer sensation. Emily climaxed in seconds with a convulsive pleasure so intense it blew her mind, and Anton followed, his great body jerking in explosive release.

Later when the tremors stopped Emily felt a wave of shame at her easy capitulation. She opened her eyes and lifted her hands to push at his chest; instead she found them gathered in one of his. He lifted his other hand and she felt him brush a few tendrils of hair from her forehead.

'You okay, Emily?'

'As okay as I will ever be as long as I am stuck with you.'

'Hell and damnation.' He swore. 'We had a fight yesterday. It is over, done with. The two people we were fighting over are dead—that is the reality. Now we move on.'

'The only place I want to move is out of here.' She couldn't help herself. He had cold-bloodedly deceived her, and he rubbed her up the wrong way with his blasted superior tone and his flaming arrogance.

'Your trouble is you can't admit that you want a man like me, can you?' he grated, bending his head and crushing her mouth under his. Then he pulled back to look into her eyes.

'You can't face reality, that is your problem; you want love and sweet nothings, a fairy tale, when anyone with any sense knows the love you imagine does not exist.'

He ran a hand through his rumpled hair, and swung his legs off the bed to sit looking down at her, totally unconscious of his nudity.

'Sexual chemistry brings a couple together, they marry and

after a year or two the lust is burned out, but usually there is a child to cement the union. For a man it is a natural instinct to protect the mother and child, and in most cases a moral duty that ensures a marriage lasts.'

Emily listened in growing amazement. 'Do you actually believe that?'

'Yes.' He stood up, stretching like a big, sated jungle beast, and turned to glance down at her. 'Mind you, from where I am standing I can't imagine ever not lusting after your naked body.' And he had the nerve to grin.

Emily grabbed the sheet and pulled it up over herself, blushing furiously. 'You are impossible.'

'Nothing is impossible if you try, Emily.' The amusement faded from his eyes. 'That is what marriage is all about,' he stated. 'Having realistic expectations.'

He was completely sure of himself, his powerful, virile body magnificently naked, and she could feel her insides melting just looking at him, and in that moment she realized she still loved him…always would…and it saddened and infuriated the hell out of her.

'And you're the expert? Don't make me laugh,' she snapped.

'I will certainly make you cry if you keep up this ridiculous fight. We can be civil to each other, the sex is great and we can have a good marriage, or you can turn it into a battlefield—it is up to you. I need a shower; you can join me, or make your mind up before I come back.'

There was only one answer, Emily realized.

Being civil and having sex… That was Anton's idea of a perfect marriage. She could do civil and sex, and a lot more. He had said he had not intended telling her what he thought of her father, but his temper had got the better of him. Well, maybe she could convince him he was wrong about her father.

Not now, not with a boatload of guests, but when they were finally alone.

He had said he would do anything to keep her. Maybe there was hope for their marriage, maybe he cared about her a lot more than he was prepared to admit…and pigs might fly…

The bottom line was, even if she proved her father had nothing to do with his sister, she could not escape the fact that was the main reason why Anton had married her.

Anton emerged from the bathroom and Emily hastily sat up in bed, dragging the cover up to her chin.

His only covering was a white towel slung precariously around his lean hips. And as she watched he moved to open one of the large wardrobes that covered one wall, withdrew something and turned.

'So what is it to be, Emily?' he asked, and discarded the towel, giving her a full-frontal view of his toned bronzed body, and stepped into a pair of Grigio Perla aqua shorts.

Emily recognized the brand because she had seen the James Bond movie that made them famous. On Anton they looked even better than the star of the movie. Fascinated by the sheer masculine perfection of his physique, she simply stared.

'I asked you a question.'

'What? Oh! Yes.' She was so mesmerized by the sight of him, she replied without thinking.

'Good,' was all he said as he pulled a polo shirt over his head. 'Make yourself decent. I'll send the chief steward in with your breakfast, and you can have a chat with him. He knows how the weekend works. It is a pretty casual affair, but if there is anything you want to change just tell him.'

Who was it said fascination is the very absence of thought, the denial of reasonable brain function? Emily wondered. She was so mesmerized by Anton she could not think rationally.

'I will see you on the pool deck when you are ready. Friday everyone tends to laze around until lunch. Then go ashore, the men to check out the cars and the women to shop. Later we all meet here to eat and then sail along to St Tropez for those who want to hit the Caves du Roy nightclub, a favourite among a few of our guests.'

He strolled over to the bed, and held out a credit card. 'Take this—you will need it later.'

She took the card and turned it over in her hand. Mrs Emily Diaz was the name inscribed.

She looked up. 'How did you get this so quickly?' she asked, no longer mesmerized but mad. Anton was so confident in his ability to get exactly what he wanted in life, including her, she realized bitterly.

'I arranged for the card to be forwarded here the day we married, as I did your passport,' Anton said, a hint of a satisfied smile quirking his wide mouth.

She affected a casual shrug. 'You're nothing if not thorough,' she said coolly. But inside she was seething with a mixture of emotions, from hate to love and, yes, lust, she admitted. But her overriding desire was to knock the smug look off his face.

'Thank you. But I don't need your money; I have enough of my own.'

'You won't for much longer if you insist on this confrontational attitude,' he drawled with a sardonic arch of one brow. 'Give it up, Emily. You're my wife—act like one. I'll expect you on deck in an hour to take care of our guests.'

The timely reminder of his hold over Fairfax Engineering knocked all the defiance out of her. 'Okay.'

She watched him walk out. He really was quite ruthless, and she had better not forget that. But if he thought she was going to be a meek little wife he was in for a rude awakening.

* * *

The number of gorgeous women lining the pit lane came as a shock to Emily. She would not have thought that so many women were keen on motor racing to bother coming for the time trials. She said as much to Max, and he gave her a grin.

'It is not the cars they are interested in, but the men—they are motor-racing groupies.' He chuckled. 'Pit Ponies.'

'Oh.' It had never occurred to her, but now she saw exactly what he meant. No wonder Anton was such a passionate fan of motor racing. Fast cars and fast women lined for his delectation, she thought scathingly.

Personally she hated the scene. The noise was horrendous, the choking smell of oil took her breath away, and she cast a baleful glance at Anton. He was standing by a low-slung racing car having an animated discussion about the engine with the chief mechanic. He looked almost boyish in his enthusiasm and at that moment, as if sensing her scrutiny, he turned, his dark eyes clashing with hers. He smiled and in a couple of lithe strides was beside her. 'So what do you think? Isn't this great?'

'Put it this way,' she said dryly, 'I can see now why they call it the pit. The place is full of men, noise, and stinks of oil and super-charged testosterone, and if it is all the same to you I think I'll go back to the yacht.'

He grimaced. 'You're right—it is probably not the place for a lady. Max will take you back, and I'll see you later.'

Back on the yacht, she heaved a sigh of relief when she learnt most of the guests had gone ashore. 'I'm going to change and have a swim,' she told Max and headed for the cabin.

She had spent yesterday being polite to their guests, and playing the perfect hostess. The nightclub in St Tropez had been a real eye-opener, all the beautiful people—she had recognized a famous American film star and a chart-topping singer to name just two. She had drunk champagne and smiled until her face ached and had hated every minute.

Then later when they had returned to the yacht she had vowed she would not respond to Anton. But when he had slid into bed naked and reached for her, her resolve had been strained to the limit. His kiss had been hungry, possessive, and passionate. She had tried to resist, her hands curling into fists at her side. But when he had lifted his head, and caught the strap of her flimsy nightgown and moved it down to palm her breast, a groan had escaped her.

'Give it up, Emily,' he said harshly. 'You know you want to.'

He was right, shaming but true…

Now with Anton on shore she felt not exactly relaxed, but at least in control for the first time in two days. Slipping into a shockingly brief black bikini, courtesy of Helen, she headed for the swimming pool. She lathered her body with sun lotion, and was wondering how to do her back when Gianni appeared, and did it for her.

Anton stepped out of the helicopter, and took the stairs two at a time to the lower deck. He was feeling great, fired up… His passion for motor racing had been fulfilled with a day in the pit watching the time trials for tomorrow's big race. The team he supported had pole position. He flexed his shoulders…and soon his other passion would be fulfilled with Emily.

She had appeared to accept his take on marriage without further argument, and yesterday she had proved to be a hit with their guests.

Last night had been incredible; his body stirred thinking about it. He had climbed into bed, taken her in his arms and kissed her. At first she had tried to play it cool, but within minutes she had gone up in flames just as she had every time before.

Yes, life was just about perfect… He needed a shower. Maybe Emily would be in the cabin. She wasn't and, ten minutes later, dressed in shorts and shirt, he walked out on deck looking for her. Carlo was leaning over the guard rail with Tim Harding and Max beside him, but there was no sign of Emily.

Anton strolled over. 'Hi, guys.' He leant against the railing next to him. 'Have you seen Emily around?'

Max pointed to a small yacht anchored about two hundred metres away. 'She is over there with Gianni. Apparently the boat belongs to friends of his and the pair of them decided to race each other across and back. They arrived there twenty minutes ago.'

The feel-good factor vanished. He felt as if he had been punched in the stomach and realized it was gut-wrenching fear. His impulse was to dive off after them, but he realized it was pointless, and then blind rage engulfed him and he turned on Max.

'You let my wife dive thirty feet off the bloody yacht,' he swore. 'Are you mad? You are supposed to be a bodyguard.'

He stilled, his chest tightening as he recognized the source of his rage. He felt an overwhelming need to protect Emily, something he had never felt for any other woman except his mother and sister.

'Sorry, boss, I couldn't stop them. They were balancing on the rail when I came out on deck. But you have nothing to worry about. Emily swims like a fish. In fact the three of us still can't decide which one won.'

'That is why we are waiting here to see them come back,' Carlo said. 'We have a little bet on the result.'

Anton could not believe his ears. 'Forget your damn bet. Nobody is swimming back. I am getting the launch.'

Carlo lifted a pair of binoculars to his eyes. 'Too late.'

Anton looked across just in time to see two figures dive into the sea.

He'd kill her; he'd shake her till her teeth rattled. He'd chain her to him… But first he needed her back safely. A boat could cut across her path, she might get cramp—the opportunity for disaster loomed huge in his mind and with bated breath he watched with Carlo and Max as the swimmers drew closer.

Reluctantly he had to admit Emily was superb. She glided through the water with barely a ripple, her long pale arms rising and falling in a perfect crawl, keeping a punishing speed. He watched as they approached the stern and saw Emily grab the ladder first.

'I won,' Emily cried, hanging onto the ladder with one hand and brushing the hair from her eyes. Gianni's arm came up and grasped her waist.

'OK—so it is one all.'

Breathless and grinning, they scrambled up onto the deck.

Anton stood transfixed. Emily, wearing the briefest of bikinis, stood glowing with life and vitality laughing with Gianni. Jealousy ripped through him and he had to battle the urge to rush across and shove the younger man overboard.

'Best of three. I'll race you tomorrow,' he heard Gianni say and his wife was totally oblivious of him as she responded.

'Right, you're on.'

Anton moved to grab Emily, but Carlo's hand on his arm stopped him. He looked up at him and said softly, 'So, my friend, now you know how it feels?'

'What do you mean?' Anton demanded.

'You know Emily and Gianni are just friends, as I know you and Eloise are just friends. But when you love a woman it doesn't always follow that you can easily accept her male friendships. Take my advice—don't make an issue out of their harmless fun.'

Carlo's words gave him pause for thought. Of course he did not love Emily. But he knew Carlo imagined he loved Eloise, and it had never occurred to him his friendship with Eloise might hurt Carlo.

Then again he wasn't Carlo, and Emily wasn't having fun with anyone but him...

'You will not be racing tomorrow, Emily.' He strode across and took her arm. 'And you, Gianni, will not encourage my wife to risk her life in such a damn-fool way.'

'Oh, don't be such an old fuddy-duddy,' Emily said, lifting her eyes to his. 'You have your motor racing. I prefer a more natural race.'

He felt every one of his thirty-seven years and he did not appreciate the reminder. His dark eyes narrowed on her beautiful face. 'Have you forgotten tomorrow we are all attending the Grand Prix? And Gianni is leaving on Monday so it is never going to happen,' he said bluntly.

'Oh, yes.' She turned away from him. 'Excuse me all, I need to shower and get ready for the party.' And he had to let her go, as Tim Harding asked him a question about the time trials.

Coloured lights strung from prow to stern lit up the great yacht. Dinner was a buffet as the original guests had been increased by about another thirty from shore. Apparently another tradition of her indomitable husband. She glanced across to where he stood surrounded by friends, mostly of the female variety. He was wearing a white shirt open at the neck and dark trousers, and looked devastatingly attractive. The dress code for the men appeared to be smart casual, actually designer casual, Emily amended, glancing around, but her eyes were helplessly drawn back to her husband.

As she watched he laughed down at the woman hanging on his arm, and Emily looked away. Anton was always going to be the centre of attention, the outstanding Alpha male, in what she quietly conceded was quite a gathering of such men. But then why not? Monaco was the playground of the rich and famous and never more so than this weekend.

'Hi, Emily.' She glanced at Gianni as he stopped beside her. 'May I say you look wicked,' he said with undisguised appreciation in his golden eyes. 'Mind you, I think you are wasted on this crowd. What say we do a bunk to my friend's yacht?'

But before she could respond Carlo appeared in front of them. 'Damn Eloise. That woman could shop for Peru,' he declared, exasperation in his tone. 'You do know she only arrived back ten minutes ago—the helicopter had to go and pick her up, hopelessly late as usual.' He snorted. 'She said it wouldn't take a minute to change.' And grasping a glass of champagne as a waiter walked by, he added, 'I will believe that when I see it.'

Gianni responded with, 'Here she comes now, Dad.'

Emily's mouth fell open in shock. The woman was wearing a white off-the-shoulder dress that revealed her breasts almost to the nipples—not that it mattered as the fabric was see-through, a silver belt was slung around her hips, and the rest of the garment barely covered her behind. Emily glanced up at Gianni and saw the slight tinge of embarrassment on his handsome young face and she felt for him.

'New dress?' Carlo demanded and Emily's attention returned to him. His eyes were popping out on stalks. He had obviously not seen it before, she surmised, and her lips twitched in the briefest of smiles. Not that there was much to see other than the fact the woman was also wearing a thong. Outrageous didn't even begin to describe it.

'No, darling.' Eloise pouted. 'You told me to hurry so I just flung this old thing on.' She preened, doing a twirl.

'She obviously missed,' Emily said under her breath to

Gianni. His golden eyes widened and he cracked up with laughter, as did Emily.

'Oh, Emily.' He flung an arm around her shoulder. 'You are priceless.' He offered between guffaws, 'And so right.'

Anton broke off mid-sentence in a rather serious discussion he was having with the Swiss banker, his attention diverted at the sound of Emily's uninhibited laughter. Her head was thrown back, revealing the long line of her throat and the upper curves of her breast; her blonde hair fell in a silken curtain almost to her waist. The dress she was wearing was red and strapless and faithfully followed every curve of her body to flare out at thigh level and end just above her knees. She looked drop-dead gorgeous and as he watched Gianni's arm went around her.

In a few lithe strides Anton was at her side. 'I am all for you enjoying yourself, Gianni,' he drawled, 'but not with my wife.'

He reached down and caught her hand as Gianni's arm fell from her shoulders.

Surprised, Emily raised laughing eyes to her husband's face and was struck by the deadly warning in the black depths of his, and looked away.

Gianni said nothing, but moved back a step; the look in Anton's eyes had said it all.

'I said be civil.' Anton slid a hand around the nape of her neck and tilted back her head so she had no choice but to look up at him. 'Not flirt with the guests and make a spectacle of yourself. What was so funny anyway?' He was jealous—not an emotion he had ever suffered from before—and he was fed up as he saw all expression drain from her face.

'You had to be there at the time to appreciate it,' she said, 'but I take your point and I am sorry. I will endeavour to be civil at all times.' And she smiled.

A perfect social smile that didn't reach her eyes.

He kept her by his side for the rest of the evening, and later in bed he utilized every bit of control and skill he possessed to drain every drop of response from her incredible body. Only when she lay exhausted and sated in his arms was he satisfied.

He gazed down at her. She had been helpless in the throes of passion as he had brought her to the knife-edge of pleasure time after time, and had held her there shuddering and writhing until finally he had possessed her completely and she had convulsed in wave after wave of excruciating delight.

Then he had started again.

She was his… He had exactly what he wanted. He frowned slightly. So what was niggling at the back of his mind? Surely not conscience… No—something else. It would come to him later, he assured himself before sleep overcame him.

The following night Emily stood in front of the floor-to-ceiling mirror in their cabin and studied her reflection. She was wearing the one floor-length gown she had packed and she grimaced. Blue shot through with silver, the halter neck left her shoulders and back bare down to her waist, and the plunging neck revealed more than a glimpse of cleavage. The rest clung to her body like a second skin. A side slit enabled her to move. When she had bought the dress it had been with her honeymoon in mind. For Anton's eyes only. Because she had loved him, even after their argument she had still harboured a lingering hope of convincing him he was wrong about her father, and making him care for her. Not any more. Once trust was destroyed there was no going back.

She had no illusions left regarding her arrogant husband. Last night he had taught her what an avid sensualist she was, and she had relished the lesson. He had driven her to the erotic height of pleasure and beyond until it had almost been pain. He was a magnificent lover.

Today she had had her relatively inexperienced opinion verified...

They had all gone to watch the Grand Prix at the home of a friend of Anton's. Settled on a long terrace overlooking the race with their guests and some more friends of the owner, Anton had asked if she minded if he went to the pits. She had bit her tongue on the caustic comment *he was the pits*. Deciding she still loved him had not lessened her feeling of betrayal. But deep inside she had still held a faint hope that their marriage might work and instead she said, 'Not at all.'

Bored out of her skull watching cars roar past at intervals, she drank a couple of glasses of champagne. And then went inside to stretch her legs. She was standing behind a huge column admiring a sculpture set in an alcove when she heard the click of heels on the marble floor and a cut-glass English voice mention her name.

'Emily Diaz has my sympathy. He is incredibly wealthy, a handsome devil, and great in the sack, as I know from personal experience. But, let's face it, the man is not marriage material. I mean, bringing her here for her honeymoon, with over a dozen guests for company—how crass is that? I couldn't believe it when we arrived. But then we never knew he had married. Heaven help the poor girl, is what I say. She seems a really nice woman, well bred by all accounts and far too good for him. I bet she has no idea that he has had affairs with at least two of us on board and probably more.'

Staying out of sight, Emily recognized the voice as the footsteps faded away. It was Sally, the wife of Tim Harding, and Emily's humiliation was complete. She had known about Eloise, but to discover another of his ex-lovers was on board was beyond belief.

That any man could be so incredibly insensitive as to invite one ex-lover on his honeymoon was the stuff of nightmares, but two… She had more or less accepted Anton's version of why Carlo and Eloise were guests…but not any more. This latest revelation was the last straw.

At that moment something finally died in Emily.

Thinking about the conversation now, Emily briskly turned away from the mirror, slipped her feet into silver stiletto sandals, and straightened up.

CHAPTER SEVEN

'YOU look incredible.'

Emily hadn't heard Anton enter, and turned slowly to face him. 'Thank you.' He was still wearing the same chinos and a polo shirt he had worn all day, and he was still grinning. The team he had sponsored had won, and the driver was now leading the world championship race and Anton had been in a celebratory mood ever since.

But then he won at everything, Emily thought sourly, but at least while he was celebrating on deck, with the other men on board, it had given her the chance to slip away.

'But a bit premature.' His hooded gaze raked over her with blatant masculine appreciation, and the eyes he lifted to hers were gleaming with a hot sensuality she could not fail to recognize as he stepped closer. 'I was hoping we could share a shower.'

'Too late.' She forced a smile, and cursed the curl of heat in her stomach his suggestion had ignited. 'I thought as this is your guests' last night, I should make an appearance at the cocktail hour, before we go ashore to the party, so if you will excuse me.' She moved to walk past him, but he caught her arm.

His lips curved in a wry smile. 'You're right, of course—the perfect hostess. I can wait, and I won't spoil your lip gloss.'

His head dipped and he brushed his lips against her brow. 'But I have something for you.'

She watched as he crossed to a small safe set in the wood-panelled wall of the cabin and withdrew a velvet-covered box.

'I meant to give you this on our wedding night,' he declared, moving to her side. 'But I was distracted.' And he opened the box to withdraw a sparkling diamond necklace. 'You might like to wear it tonight.'

Emily glanced at the necklace, and reached out to stop his hand as he would have slipped it around her neck, and took it from him.

'Thank you. It is beautiful.' She let the waterfall of diamonds run through her fingers, and slowly raised her eyes to his. 'But unfortunately it is not right for this gown.' She handed it back to him. 'I'll wear it some other time.'

It was a first for Anton, a woman rejecting his gift, not just any woman but his wife… How dared she? Grim-faced, he scanned Emily's exquisite features and slowly it dawned on him while he thought they had had a great day, his wife did not share his enthusiasm. He had given her a fortune in diamonds and yet she looked singularly unimpressed. No woman of his acquaintance would have dreamt of doing that—usually they fell over themselves in gratitude. But Emily had actually handed them back to him.

'If you say so.' He placed the necklace back in the box and returned it to the safe, and when he turned back Emily had fastened something around her neck, and was slipping a bracelet on her wrist.

Anton moved towards her and stopped. Her long blonde hair was swept back in a smooth knot on top of her head, the severity of the style emphasizing the perfect symmetry of her delicate features. The shimmering blue dress caressed her superb body like a lover's hand. The simple tie at the back of her neck left the shoulders bare and revealed the silken-smooth skin of her straight back almost to her waist. But it was the platinum chain with a heart-shaped diamond and sapphire-encrusted locket suspended between the creamy soft curves of her breasts that captured all his attention.

'Nice pendant.' He reached out and fingered the locket and wondered who had bought it for her. Maybe her ex-fiancé? Not that it mattered, he wasn't jealous…he was never jealous…he was just curious, he told himself.

'Yes, I like it,' she said and, stepping back, she added, 'and I have the bracelet to match.'

She held out her wrist for his approval. The heart motif was followed in a string of diamonds with smaller sapphire centres around her slender wrist.

'I have never seen you wear them before.' He wasn't going to ask her… But he did. 'Who gave them to you?'

Emily glanced up at him. So far Anton had got all his own way in this farce of a marriage, but not any more, and she took great delight in telling him.

'The locket was a present from my parents for my eighteenth birthday. And the bracelet was a present from my father on my twenty-first birthday. Beautiful, aren't they? And surprisingly they match the ring you bought me. Isn't that fortuitous?'

Anton frowned at the mention of her father, though, if he was honest, in a way he was relieved. 'Yes, very,' he agreed. Better a father than the ex-fiancé he had imagined.

She turned to leave, and he caught her wrist. 'Wait.'

'Was there something else?' Her eyes flicked over him.

'No, not really.' It was not like him to be so indecisive. But there was something… She was as exquisite as ever, as polite, but the blue eyes that met his no longer revealed her every thought. Instead, he realized, they looked cold, almost cynical…

He let go of her hand and she left.

Was he responsible for the change in Emily, her cynicism? he wondered for a moment. He shrugged his shoulders. No... In his experience all women were notoriously volatile; wrong time of the month, wrong clothes—anything could upset them. Problem resolved, he headed for the shower.

Emily looked around her. Not only did it make it easier for her to ignore Anton's hand resting lightly on her waist, it enabled her to study the glittering throng, or, if she was honest, the women.

Anton was at home in this crowd. He had introduced her to the winning owner of the team, and a host of other people whose names she didn't even try to remember. But all the time in the back of her mind was the nagging question if he could invite two of his ex-girlfriends to stay with them for the weekend, how many more of the women here had he slept with?

By Anton's own admission he had been attending the Monaco Grand Prix for years, and she had not forgotten what Max had told her about the 'Pit Ponies'. What a degrading nickname for female groupies, and what did it say about the men who used them? Her husband probably one.

'So, Emily, have you had enough?' Anton said softly. 'Want to go back to the yacht?' She felt the warmth of his breath against her ear and tensed.

His hand tightened on her waist and the warmth of his long body against hers was a temptation, a temptation she was determined to resist.

'No.' She looked up at his brutally handsome face. His dark eyes held a wealth of sensual knowledge that excited and shamed her.

'Actually, I would like to go to the casino,' she said sweetly. 'Carlo told me you usually all go after the party—it is another tradition of yours, apparently.' Along with bedding any beautiful female he fancied, she almost added…

Anton cursed Carlo under his breath, and, much as he ached to get Emily back in bed, he could not deny her the trip. He had already taken all the eye-rolling and ribbing he could stand from his motor-sport acquaintances when he had introduced her as his wife, when Emily had quite blithely told them this was his idea of a honeymoon. 'Yes, okay.'

Anton gritted his teeth as the roulette wheel spun again.

'Oh, my God!' Emily exclaimed as the white ball landed on her age, number twenty-four, on the roulette wheel. 'I've won again.'

The croupier gave her a broad smile and shoved a huge stack of chips towards her, and Anton wanted to shove him in the face.

'Yes, Emily,' he said, stopping her hand as she went to place another bet. 'But we have been here over three hours. The others left ages ago. You have won at least ten thousand, so don't push your luck.'

The euphoria of his team's win, his earlier good mood had totally evaporated and slowly he had begun to realize that Emily was delaying going back to the yacht. Trying to avoid going to bed with him. Well, not any more; she enjoyed sex with an appetite that matched his own, and he had waited long enough.

She cast him a look. 'Have I really? That rather proves the maxim—lucky at cards, unlucky in love.' And she gave him a brittle smile.

'Cut out the sarcasm. Collect your chips—we are leaving.'

He was angry. She had with very little persuasion been a willing bed partner after their original argument. She had agreed to continue their marriage in a civilized manner. He could not fault her—she had been perfectly polite to their guests, if a bit sarcastic to him at times, which he could understand given her upset over her father and the honeymoon, he silently conceded. But he wasn't a fool. Now there was definitely something else bugging her…

He was sure of it when they finally got back to their cabin and he drew her into his arms.

She tried to pull away from him, but he merely tightened his hold on her and looked down at her with smouldering eyes.

'I have waited all night for this,' he said, and bent his head to take her mouth. But she averted her face and his lips brushed her cheek.

'Do you mind, Anton, but it is four in the morning and after the last few hectic days I am exhausted.' Her eyes avoided his, and her body stiffened in his arms. 'Plus I need to be up in a few hours—a couple of your guests are leaving early.'

'One kiss.' He grasped the nape of her neck and tipped back her head; she closed her eyes, and parted her lips, and he kissed her.

He kept on kissing her until she was melting in his arms. Then he lifted his head, and stared down into her flushed face. No woman manipulated him with sex, never had, never would.

'Are you sure you are too tired?' he drawled mockingly.

She looked at him for a long moment, and he could actually see her withdrawal, the sensuality fading from her eyes, freezing him out.

'Yes, sorry,' she apologized, and slipped out of his arms. 'But don't let me stop you. I have it on good authority there are at least two other women you have slept with on board. I'm sure one will oblige. If not you could always nip ashore and pick up a motor-racing groupie with no trouble at all.'

Anton stiffened in outrage, and for a moment he said nothing as he fought to control the fury that surged through him at her insult to his moral integrity, his dark eyes narrowing to slits as he took in her cool face.

'That is some opinion you have of me, Emily, and in the future I might take up your generous offer,' he drawled. 'But first I'd like to know who fed you such lies?'

'Well, I knew about Eloise, of course, but while you were doing your man thing with cars I overheard Sally Harding describing your incredible sexual skill in the bedroom, and pitying me because what man would be so crass as to invite, I believe her exact words were *at least* two of his ex-lovers on his honeymoon.'

Her explanation was delivered in such a cool, disinterested voice that Anton simply glared at her. He did not trust himself to speak—disgust and anger washing over him.

'And you believed her?' he finally demanded through gritted teeth.

She gave him a derisory glance. 'The number of women you have bedded is legendary according to the press and I don't hear you denying it.'

His reputation in the business world was first class, and he would defend it to the hilt. But he had never concerned himself with the vastly exaggerated claims the press made about the women in his life.

'I don't have to,' he snapped. 'As for Sally Harding, she is a married woman who came on to me. A woman scorned and all that.'

'If you say so.' She shrugged her shoulders and Anton saw the patent disbelief in her face as she turned and disappeared into the bathroom, slamming the door behind her.

He stepped forward, his knee-jerk reaction to go after her, convince her of the truth. Then he stopped, masculine pride coming to the fore. He had never seen the need to justify himself to a woman in his life and he was not going to start now. It smacked too much of begging…

It was another new experience for Anton. No woman had ever rejected him and *apologized*. Then insulted him so thoroughly that he was still having difficulty believing Emily…his wife of mere days…had casually suggested he seek out another woman for sex.

The anger he had held in check for so long engulfed him. A string of Spanish expletives rolled off his tongue, and in a mood as black as thunder he stalked out of the cabin and up on deck. He did not trust himself to be around Emily right now without losing control, and that was unthinkable…

When he had cooled down and returned Emily was curled up in bed fast asleep.

She was so innocent and so gullible, the Harding woman had probably known Emily was listening and had fed her a pack of lies. She was no match for some of the female sharks that moved in the circle of the super-rich, or for the news hounds that preyed on a man in his position.

Given his family background, he had learnt long ago that it was pointless issuing denials—it only added fuel to the flames of gossip. Any woman he was seen with was automatically labelled his latest mistress. Yet he had never actually kept a mistress in the true sense of the word. The knowledge of his mother's not particularly happy life spent waiting for a man to visit, a second-class lover, and for her son a virtually non-existent father, was a salutary lesson.

Sure, as a single, healthy, sexually active male, of course there had been women in his life, women he had had relationships with lasting from a few months to over a year, though he had never lived with a woman. He preferred his own space. But they were women he respected and when the inevitable parting had come, they had for the most part remained friends. In fact he could count them on his fingers, and he had only once had a one-night stand and that had been with Eloise, and a disaster. Whether Emily would believe him was questionable. But whatever her father had done to his sister, he realized, revenge and pride aside, it was up to him to reassure her. She deserved that much.

Quietly he stripped and showered, then slid into bed beside her. He looped an arm around her waist and drew her into his body. She didn't stir and for a long time he lay with Emily enfolded in his arms. She was his…and he could set her straight in the morning, was his last arrogant thought as he drifted off to sleep.

Emily stood at Anton's side as they waved farewell to the last of their guests, the picture of marital bliss, she thought, when nothing could be further from the truth.

She flinched as Anton's hands cupped her shoulders and he turned her to face him. 'So, Emily, where would you like to go? I have to be in New York next Monday, but we have a week to do what you want. We can cruise anywhere in the Mediterranean or we can go to my Greek island villa, whichever you prefer.'

She glanced up at him; his dark eyes held hers and she knew what he was thinking. She had awakened this morning wrapped in his arms, and their early morning love-making was a potent sensual memory simmering between them. No, sex session, she amended with a now familiar dull ache in the region of her heart.

Afterwards he had explained why Sally Harding had lied—apparently she had come on to him a couple of years ago and Anton had knocked her back. Her husband was a friend of his. He also told her that naturally there had been a few other women in his life. But if he had slept with the number the press accredited him with he would never have made a fortune and would have been dead from exhaustion by now. Emily had said she believed him, because lying sated beneath him she couldn't have done much else, but she noted he never said how many! He had given her a very masculine satisfied smile and a tender, but in Emily's opinion vaguely condescending, kiss.

It was amazing to her how a brilliantly clever, highly successful man in the business world could so completely separate the physical from the emotional when it came to his sex life.

She could not do it... But she was trapped, and not just by worry over her family. She was trapped by her helpless desire for him. It was like a fever in her blood. She had thought after what she had discovered yesterday that she was cured of her helpless response to him. But this morning he had proved her wrong.

He had awakened her with a kiss, she had tried to resist, she had hit out at him, and tried to wriggle from beneath him, but he had simply pinned her down with his great body and had the audacity to laugh at her feeble attempt to dislodge him. 'So you want to play rough, hmm?' he had drawled, and kissed her again, his strong hands roaming over her body, finding erogenous zones she never knew she had, until the fire in her blood overwhelmed her, and she was reaching for him...kissing him...

She knew every day she spent with him she would just fall deeper under his sensual spell. She could not resist him, and he knew it. Before she had had no idea sex could become so addictive, but she did now. She craved his touch and it filled her with shame and seriously dented her self-esteem.

Max had left earlier with the guests and, alone now apart from the crew, paradoxically the yacht seemed smaller. Spending a week with no escape from the vessel filled her with alarm. At least on land there was the possibility of walking away from Anton for a while, escaping the overwhelming physical attraction he held for her. On the yacht there was nowhere to hide...

'I suppose home is out of the question,' she said with an edge of sarcasm.

'Your home is with me. Decide or I will decide for you.'

His hands tightened on her shoulders and she saw the ruthless implacability in his dark eyes. 'In that case your villa sounds nice.'

'Good. I will inform the captain. Unfortunately I have some work that can't wait. Amuse yourself for a while, and try the pool.' He drew her to him and kissed her with a possessive passion that made her senses swim and, lifting his head, he added, 'I'll catch you later, and that is a promise.'

By the gleam of masculine anticipation in the dark eyes that met hers she knew that was one promise he would keep.

'Okay,' she murmured, and watched him stride away. Probably the only promise he ever kept where women were concerned, Emily thought sadly.

Leaning over the rail, she recalled the promise he had made in church. It seemed like a lifetime ago now. She had meant every word of her vows, but she realized they had meant nothing to him—they had simply been a means to an end. As for his excuse about his ex-lovers...if they were ex, she amended, she didn't believe him for a moment.

Anton was a man with a very high sex-drive—even she in her innocence had gathered that in the last few days. She doubted he had even noticed the difference from their wedding night, when she had loved him freely and told him so frequently, to the silent lover she had forced herself to become. If it wasn't her he was having sex with it would be some other woman.

The thought caused her pain, and with the pain came a hint of an idea, maybe a way out...

Anton was an incredibly wealthy man, and yet by some oversight he had never suggested she sign a pre-nup. Or, more likely in his conceit, his supreme confidence in his ability to keep her sexually satisfied, and with the lavish lifestyle he offered, he probably didn't think he needed one.

But the likelihood of him staying faithful to her or any woman wasn't very great. Suddenly it occurred to her all she had to do was wait. He had said she could carry on with her career, and his took him all over the world. Inevitably they would spend a lot of time apart; she could make sure of it. Once, only once, would she need to discover he had been with another woman, and she could divorce him. Then take rather a lot of his money, at least enough to make sure he could never threaten her family ever again.

It was a horrible cynical idea and not like her at all, but then living with a cynic like Anton it was hardly surprising she was learning to think like him.

In fact she could take a leaf out of his book, and spend the time on his island indulging the sexual side of her nature, a side she had never known she had before. He had said it was just lust that brought a couple together, and eventually it burnt out. Well, by the end of the week, her body sated, she might finally be rid of her helpless longing for him, or at least better able to control herself.

Yes, she decided. She would do it—make the rest of her honeymoon a sensual feast even though the marriage was a fiasco.

Washed and dressed in shorts and a tee shirt, Emily walked downstairs and out onto the veranda where breakfast was laid out. Anton had already eaten, by the look of it. He had left their bed to take an urgent call an hour or so ago. Where he was now, she didn't know.

She crossed to the balustrade and stood admiring the view. The villa was set on the top of a hill that overlooked a beautiful bay; the gardens ran down in a riot of colour almost to the beach, the white sand reaching out to the deep green sea. Around the headland she knew was a small harbour and fishing village, because that was where they had docked yesterday afternoon. But here it felt as if she were the only person in the world.

A hand wrapped around her waist and settled on her stomach, urging her back into the warmth of a large male body.

'So do you like my home?' Anton's deep voice rumbled against her ear.

'Like is too tame a word—this place is like paradise.' Or it could be under different circumstances, she silently amended.

The villa was beautiful with five bedrooms, three reception rooms, a study and a circular, elegant hall with a marble staircase. Not excessively large, but with a basement gym and games room, and fabulous terraced gardens including an infinity swimming pool. A staff of four ensured the house ran like clockwork, and a team of gardeners kept the grounds in perfect condition. The place had everything; much like the man who owned it, she thought, and inwardly sighed.

'Good. So what do you want to do today?'

'Explore, swim in the sea,' she said, wriggling around in his arms, and placing her hands firmly on his chest. 'So far I have only seen the harbour when we arrived, the house and the bedroom suite.'

'Your wish is my command.' He grinned, and half an hour later they were driving along a narrow road in an open-topped Jeep, Anton wearing the most disreputable pair of cut-off jeans that bordered on the indecent and nothing else, Emily with a baseball cap on her head at Anton's insistence, her arms and legs liberally covered in sunblock.

The Jeep screeched to an abrupt halt at the harbour, Anton leapt out and before Emily could move he had reached over and lifted her to the ground.

'First I'll take you for the best cup of coffee in the world, but don't tell my housekeeper I said that.' He chuckled, and pulled out a chair for her by a rickety table outside a small café.

Immediately the owner came out, and Emily's eyes widened in surprise as the man greeted Anton with a bear hug, and hearing Anton speaking in Greek, so obviously at home, she felt her heart squeeze a little. She was introduced to the owner, coffee was served, with small sweet-tasting cakes, and as they sat there the entire population of the village must have walked by and she was introduced to them all, old and young alike.

This was an Anton she had never seen before, laughing, chatting and totally relaxed.

'Come.' He reached down a hand to her. 'Time to explore.'

They spent the day driving around the island, which actually did not take long. They lunched on bread and cheese, high up in the centre of the island as guests of a goat-herder that Anton knew, and then spent the afternoon down on a secluded beach.

Anton stepped out of his disreputable shorts, and, totally naked, persuaded her to do the same. They swam and laughed and Emily discovered it was possible to have sex in the sea. Finally they returned to the villa as the sun was setting, Emily slightly sunburnt and covered in sand, Anton looking more bronzed and fit than ever. They shared a shower, dined on the veranda and had an early night.

It was the honeymoon she had hoped for, and, even though she knew it was a sham, Emily shed all her inhibitions and enjoyed every second. She knew she would never love another man the way she had loved Anton, and with that in mind she blocked every negative thought from her brain. One week of sensual bliss was what she had promised herself, and amazingly it was.

CHAPTER EIGHT

'SO WHAT would you like to do for your last day?' Anton asked, letting his eyes rest on Emily. She had pushed her chair back from the table, and was sitting with her long legs stretched out before her, cradling a cup of coffee in her hands, her gaze fixed on the garden and sea below.

She turned her head slightly. 'I thought I might have a swim in the pool, and then pack.'

God! But she was stunning. She positively glowed, a golden girl in every respect. The whole population of the island adored her; she was fun and friendly to everyone. She had obviously got over their argument about her father and that stupid Harding woman. But then he had always known she would after a week in his bed, he thought complacently.

Actually, he had never spent a better week in his life. She was his perfect match, in bed and out, and more than he could ever have wished for. She was wearing a flesh-coloured bikini with a fine sarong loosely draped around her and fastened with a knot between her breasts, and he felt his body stirring even though it wasn't long since they had indulged in the shower. Actually, for an innocent she had surprisingly seductive taste in lingerie, he realized, but then she was naturally sensuous, and so long as it was for his eyes only not a problem.

'Then I suppose I better make arrangements for a flight.'

Lost in contemplation of her body and what he wanted to do with it, Anton almost missed the rest of her reply. Regrouping his thoughts, he corrected her. 'No need, that is all taken care of. The helicopter will pick us up tomorrow morning and take us to Athens where my jet is waiting.'

She looked at him quizzically. 'Oh, but I thought you were going to work in New York.'

'Yes, I am.'

'Well, I have to be back in London for Tuesday. I have arranged to see some special, very fragile documents at the maritime museum to help in my research, and you did say I could carry on with my career.'

Anton's face darkened momentarily. Yes…he had said that, but that was before… Before what? Before he had developed an insatiable desire for her…

Maybe it was best he went to New York alone. He had meetings lined up all day every day and Emily was too much of a distraction. No…his nights were free and Emily could amuse herself during the day. He had never known a woman who did not love shopping and New York was a shopper's paradise.

'Yes, I did. But you have never been to my penthouse in London before. I need to accompany you the first time, clear you with Security, and introduce you to the staff,' he explained airily. 'It will be much more convenient if you reschedule your research for a later date, when we can go to London together. You will like New York, and while I work you can shop to your heart's content.'

Convenient for whom? Emily wondered dryly. He was so arrogant, so confident she would fall in with his plans like a meek little wife, and she had no intention of playing along.

She had enjoyed the week living in a fool's paradise. The

long days in the sun and the equally long steamy nights of sex—
she had indulged the sensual side of her nature to the nth degree.
It had not been difficult—Anton relaxed and among plain-
living island people was a different person.

They had laughed and talked about anything and everything.
He had told her how his Spanish Peruvian grandmother had
ended up a madam in a voice filled with affection, and no re-
crimination. Apparently when her lover had disappeared a few
months after his mother was born, a bitter enemy of her es-
tranged father had proposed an arrangement beneficial to both
of them. He had needed someone to front a high-class brothel
he owned, which his family had naturally known nothing about.
No sex was involved, he had assured her. It had been enough
for him that her father's name via his unmarried daughter was
very publicly discredited twice over... She had had nothing
more to lose and accepted.

To Emily, Anton's past went some way to explaining why
he had been so determined she should share his name, Diaz.
Polite society was hard on what was seen as immoral, most
would say rightly so. Anton was a fiercely proud man and,
though she knew he would never admit the past history of his
family affected him in any way, deep down as a young boy in
Peru he must have suffered for it. He was half Greek and yet
she realized he was probably more Peruvian than anything
else. He had freely admitted his work was his life and his only
other great interest was breeding horses at his ranch in Peru.

They had swum naked in the sea and made love whenever
the mood arose, which was pretty much constantly. But now it
had to end, because underneath, in her few solitary moments,
and even understanding a little better why he behaved as he did,
she still could not forgive or forget the main reason he had
married her, and, based on a lie, it had nothing to do with love.

'I am not keen on shopping and I can easily stay with Tom and Helen,' she finally answered.

She saw him stiffen, his darkly handsome face suddenly grim. No, he didn't like that… In his masculine conceit he thought he knew everything about her, but actually all he knew was her name and body.

'I'll be fine, and you don't need to worry,' she continued conversationally. 'I will not tell Tom and Helen the real reason you married me. There is no point in upsetting them by repeating your lies about Dad.' She rose to her feet. 'But I think I will go and book my flight before my swim.'

'No.' Anton shot up, and caught her wrist. 'I did not lie about your father, damn you, and I have a letter to prove it,' he snapped. That she could once again try to defy him after the perfect week they had shared puzzled and enraged him.

'I'll believe that when I see it,' she said with the delicate arch of one brow.

'You will—believe me,' he opined hardly.

'If you say so.' She shrugged her shoulders. 'But for all I know your sister could have lied.' She was being deliberately insulting and it pained her to do it, but she needed to make the break. She lifted wide blue eyes to his. 'After all, she was certainly no Mother Teresa, if as you say she was single and got pregnant at eighteen, a trait that seems to run in your family.' His dark eyes blazed and for a second she thought he was going to hit her.

Instead he twisted her wrist behind her back and hauled her hard against him. His mouth crashed down on hers in a deeply savage kiss that was more punishment than passion. She shuddered and he lifted his head, his dark eyes blazing down into hers.

'Hell, what's got into you? I thought…'

'What did you think?' She gasped. 'That your expertise in

the bedroom would make me forget why you married me? Well, sorry, it hasn't and it never will.' It took every shred of self-control she possessed to continue. 'You said civil and sex. And civil and sex is what you get. I need to be in London by Tuesday to continue with my career as agreed,' she reminded him emphatically.

She felt his hands tighten and then she was free. He stepped back and looked at her for a long moment with narrowed eyes, and then he gave her a dry smile.

'You're right, of course. But we will have to spend some time in the next few hours comparing schedules. I have no intention of being a celibate husband,' he drawled sardonically.

He reached out and she flinched, but all he did was tuck a stray tendril of hair behind her ear. 'And as for booking a flight, Emily—forget it.' His hand lingered for a moment on her nape. 'Go have your swim; one of the maids can pack for you. We will leave after lunch. I will see you safely settled in the London apartment and fly on to America tomorrow morning from England—it makes no difference to me.'

She looked at him quizzically. Such an about-face was unlikely from what she knew of him. But his expression was unreadable; he looked curiously detached.

'Do you really mean that?' she asked.

'Of course. Obviously the honeymoon, such as it was, is over. There is not much point in spending another night here.'

'Well, thank you.'

'You can thank me properly later. I need to call my pilot.' And, turning, he walked away.

Lunch was set out on the veranda overlooking the gardens, but there was no sign of Anton. Emily picked desultorily at a few bits of cold meat. She wasn't hungry. The maid appeared with a message from Anton. He was too busy to join her and had requested a tray in his study. He had also told her to inform Emily to be ready to leave in an hour.

Emily walked down the stairs exactly an hour later; she had changed her casual clothes for the blue suit she had worn on her wedding day. A day that seemed a lifetime ago now. Anton was standing in the hall, a laptop in one hand and a cell phone in his other pressed to his ear.

She paused halfway down. He was wearing a light business suit, immaculately tailored to his long, lithe body. He looked stunning, but she could almost feel the tension in him, could hear it in the clipped, impatient tone of his voice, and she pitied the person on the other end. He was no longer the laughing companion of the past week in disreputable shorts, but the cold, remote tycoon. Well, it was what she wanted…wasn't it?

Anton turned at the sound of heels on the marble floor, his dark eyes narrowing on his wife descending the stairs. The memory of her descending the grand old staircase of Deveral Hall on their wedding day flashed in his mind. She had been wearing the same suit, her blue eyes shining with happiness and the smile on her face enough to light up the huge hall, and it had been solely focused on him.

Suddenly he recognized the difference in her that had been niggling at the back of his mind since the arrival of the guests in Monte Carlo. The sex was great, but he had never seen the same unbridled happiness in her eyes, or heard the soft cries of love and delight she had showered him with on their wedding night. This past week on his island he had thought perfect, Emily had been enthusiastic, a truly amazing lover, but apart from a few sighs and groans a very quiet one.

Not that it mattered. She was his wife, and he had got what he wanted.

So why was he not satisfied?

'Good, you're ready.' He crossed to the foot of the stairs, and at that moment a startling idea formed in his mind, the hint of a wicked smile curving his lips… 'The helicopter is waiting.'

Emily saw his smile but did not reciprocate. She simply allowed him to lead her to the waiting helicopter. The flight to Athens was smooth and they boarded Anton's private plane for England with the minimum of communication between them.

As soon as they were airborne Anton removed himself from the seat next to her and crossed to the other side of the cabin, and, seated at a table, he opened his laptop and worked.

John the steward served coffee, and, having provided her with a handful of magazines, asked if there was anything else she wanted. He was a friendly young man and chatting to him she discovered his ambition was to travel the world and this job was one way of doing so.

As for Anton, he barely glanced at her.

She flicked through a magazine, and found an article on the discovery of a new tomb in Egypt that contained the mummy of a female pharaoh that predated all the others. She read it with interest, then, closing her eyes, she allowed her mind to drift.

Was she doing the right thing insisting on returning to England? she wondered. She wasn't ready to face Tom and Helen—they knew her too well, and would quickly realize there was something wrong with her marriage. Still, she would be staying in Anton's apartment—she could quite easily keep out of their way and a few days of her own company was exactly what she needed, she concluded, and drifted off to sleep.

When she opened her eyes, some time later, she glanced out of the window…

John appeared, quietly offering her a drink, tea or alcohol, before asking if she would like to order dinner.

It was the dinner that got her attention. 'But surely we must be landing soon.' She glanced at her wrist-watch. It was a four-hour flight, and they had been in the air almost that now.

'No, we are only about halfway.'

'Halfway!' she exclaimed. 'Halfway to where?'

'New York,' John began. 'We—'

'Shut up, John, I can take it from here.' Anton appeared and, catching her arm, he lifted her to her feet, his dark eyes gleaming with devilment. 'Time to show you around, darling.'

Flushed and almost choking with anger, she stared up at him. The filthy rotten swine had told her he would take her to London and she had actually thanked him... He had lied... The barefaced audacity of the man was unbelievable. Rotting in hell was too good for him.

'Why, you arrogant lying bast—' was as far as she got before his mouth descended on her in a kiss so deep, so passionate, she could hardly breathe, and when he finally let her come up for air she was slumped weakly against him, only his strong arms wrapped around her preventing her collapsing at his feet.

'You didn't really think I would allow you to dictate to me,' he murmured with a sardonic arch of one black brow. 'No woman ever has or ever shall.'

Speechless with rage, she gazed wildly around. Of John there was no sign. And she was stuck thirty thousand feet up over the Atlantic...

'You can't do this,' she hissed. 'It is little better than kidnapping.' His hand slipped around the nape of her neck, and he tipped her head back.

'I already have,' he drawled mockingly. 'Accept it, Emily.' Curving his arm firmly around her waist, he almost frog-marched her to the cabin at the rear that housed a double bed and a shower room.

As soon as he closed the door behind them Emily tore out of his hold and spun around. 'You rotten, lying toad,' she spat, boiling with rage. 'You said…'

He snaked an arm around her waist and hauled her back against him and she lashed out wildly with hands and feet. His other hand slipped between the lapels of her jacket and cupped her breast, and he laughed, he actually laughed as he tumbled her back on the bed.

Emily tensed, her moment of rebellion over, suddenly fiercely aware of his big body sprawled on top of her, his long fingers edging beneath the lace of her bra to pluck at her hardening nipple. She groaned almost in despair, appalled by the ease with which her body, even in anger, was incapable of resisting his slightest touch.

'Anticipation can be hell, my sweet,' he said, his sensuous lips curving in a knowing smile, and she wanted to strangle him. 'But also heaven.' He brushed his mouth against hers, and inserted a long leg between her thighs.

'We have plenty of time. How do you feel about joining the mile high club?' he asked teasingly as his fingers teased her breast.

He thought this was a huge joke…and from somewhere she got the strength to grasp his wrist and tug his hand from her breast and say, 'No.' Wriggling from beneath him, she sat up, her back to him, and adjusted her clothes with trembling hands.

She wanted to scream, rant and rave in frustration at the conniving devil that was her husband. But what was the point? It would only draw the attention of the crew, and make her look a bigger idiot than she already was.

After all, what woman in her right mind would fight with a filthy-rich handsome man who had actually done her the honour of marrying her?

She flashed a furious look back at Anton; he was sprawled

on his back, his hands behind his head. He had shed his jacket and unfastened the top three buttons of his shirt. He looked relaxed, completely unaffected by their passionate encounter, while she was still trembling.

'Feel free to change your mind any time. Long flights can be so boring.' He grinned and closed his eyes. 'Wake me when you want me.'

When hell freezes over, Emily thought, furious and frustrated.

On arrival in New York they were met by Max with a limousine and driven silently to Anton's apartment overlooking Central Park. She still had trouble believing he had actually brought her to the city against her will. But then she had very little will around him, she silently conceded.

Anton ushered her out of the car into an apartment building and straight into the elevator. He pressed the button, then leant negligently against the wall, his laptop in one hand, looking at her, a brooding expression in his dark eyes.

In the close confines of the elevator she felt the tension mounting as the silence lengthened and finally she said, 'I thought Max was coming with us?'

'No, he is parking the car, and then he will deliver your luggage and leave. He has his own place here, but he will be back tomorrow afternoon.'

'He seems to spend a lot of time with you.' She'd never really thought what Max's actual job was; she supposed he was a sort of PA. 'What exactly does he do?

'Max is the head of my security and a friend I can trust.'

'You mean a bodyguard? But that's ridiculous.'

'Not ridiculous. Inconvenient at times, but a necessity in my world. I run a highly successful business and there is always some crook wanting to make easy money or a business rival wanting to cut in on a deal. Max watches and listens out for me, ready to inform me of any danger. In fact, from the day we got engaged you have also had a bodyguard.'

'You mean I have been watched all the time?' Emily declared, appalled and furious at the thought. She felt as though her privacy had been invaded along with her body and everything else in her life since she had met Anton. 'Well, I won't have it. I will not be followed around by anyone.'

He shrugged negligently. 'Max's operatives are first class and incredibly discreet. I can guarantee you won't even notice. I am an extremely wealthy man and as my wife you could be a target for kidnappers.'

'And you would certainly know all about kidnapping,' she fumed.

'Forget it, Emily. You are here and the security is not negotiable… Understood?'

She understood just fine…but she had no intention of going along with the restriction on her privacy and she had no doubt she could slip the surveillance when she wanted to. Letting none of her feelings show, she glanced coolly up at him. 'Perfectly.'

'Good. I knew you would see reason.'

Emily almost lost it then. He had to be the most confident, arrogant, egotistical man on the planet. Instead she bit her lip and said not a word…

The elevator stopped, and Anton ushered her out with a hand at her back. Involuntarily she stiffened. His hand fell away and he cast her a sardonic smile.

'The entrance is this way.' He indicated the double doors at the end of a thickly carpeted hall and walked on, leaving her trailing in his wake.

He opened the door and stepped back. 'Your new home.' He gestured for her to enter.

He followed her and introduced her to his Spanish house-keeper, Maria, and her husband, Philip, who looked after the place for him.

'I will leave Maria to show you around. I have work to catch up on.'

'Wait…may I use your telephone?' Emily asked. 'I want to ring Helen, tell her where I am.'

Anton turned back. 'You didn't bring your cell phone with you?'

He knew she had one—he had called her frequently before they were married—and she saw the surprise in his eyes. 'Oddly enough, I did not think I needed it on my honeymoon,' she sniped.

His dark eyes shadowed. 'Okay, there is no need to labour the point, Emily. I get the message. My mistake, the honeymoon was not what you expected, but then life is rarely what we expect,' he said enigmatically. 'This is your home now; feel free to use the telephone and anything else you please. But a word of advice: there is a four-hour time difference. It will be eleven in the evening in London. I doubt Helen will appreciate the call.'

'I forgot, but I would, however, like to check my e-mails. Could I borrow a computer?'

'No need. I will have one provided for you tomorrow. As for now, Maria has prepared a meal. It is better to stay awake to avoid jet lag, though I can think of better things to do than eat, but by the look on your face I doubt if you would agree,' he drawled sardonically. 'I will see you at dinner.' And with that he left.

He had the last word as usual, Emily thought bitterly.

Maria showed her around the apartment. A huge lounge and formal dining room, a day room and study. Plus three *en suite* bedrooms and an incredible master bedroom with huge *en suite* bathroom including a wet room. The floors were polished timber, the décor traditional rather than modern, and the view over New York through a wall of glass enough to take her breath away.

She returned to the master bedroom to discover Maria had unpacked her clothes, and thoughtfully brought her a cup of coffee. 'To keep you awake after big flight,' she said in her broken English.

Showered, Emily dressed in skimpy white lace bra and briefs, white harem pants and a fitted white silk top embroidered in silver. She grimaced at her reflection; she did not have a lot to choose from. Her honeymoon wardrobe was limited, and much more revealing than the clothes she usually wore.

In her day-to-day life she preferred casual clothes, but she also kept a core wardrobe of designer clothes to suit any occasion. But taking Helen's advice she had bought her trousseau with a romantic honeymoon in mind, to please her husband. More fool her, she thought, disgusted with herself for being so stupidly trusting.

Then and now—why else was she in New York instead of London?

Dinner was a tense affair. Anton asked if the apartment was to her liking, and told her if she wanted to change anything to ask Maria. He had tomorrow morning free, and he would show her something of the city.

She looked at him across the dining table. 'There is no need. I'm sure Max will be more than enough to assure I don't get lost,' she said, still fuming at being hauled here and stuck with a bodyguard.

'Give it up, Emily,' he said, exasperation in his tone. 'Tomorrow morning I am taking you out. We are going to be here a while—you will have plenty of time to explore later.'

'Why would I want to? Especially as I did not expect to be here,' she said bluntly.

'I spend a lot of time here and as my wife so will you,' he responded curtly. 'At present I am in the process of a big takeover, and in the last stages of negotiation. I have great faith in my staff but any slip-up can cost a fortune so my personal involvement is a necessity,' he explained.

'I see. A lot more important than my research, which earns you nothing,' she said sarcastically.

'Be honest, Emily.' His dark eyes hardened on her pale face. 'Your career, though interesting, is not the major part of your life. You freelance as a marine archaeologist. I know you have been on three expeditions in the Mediterranean. But basically by far the vast majority of your time has been spent in London, researching at various libraries and museums.'

Emily sat up straighter in her chair, his disparaging but clearly informed awareness of her career enough to stiffen her spine. 'And how would you know that?' she demanded.

'I had you investigated.' He shrugged.

'Of course, silly me—what else is a prospective groom to do?' She lowered her long lashes over her eyes, and stabbed at a prawn on her plate. She was hurt that he had such a dim view of what she had worked so hard to achieve over the years. Well, what was one more hurt on all the others he had heaped on her? she thought philosophically and, picking up her wineglass, she drained it.

'Emily, ignoring reality is dangerous. You are in New York now, whether you like it or not. A place you are not familiar with and you will have protection,' Anton stated, looking directly at her. 'Especially as I do spend a good deal of time here.'

'I could not live here,' Emily said firmly. 'It is too…' She paused. She had only seen the traffic on the way from the airport and the streets teeming with people. 'Fast.'

'You won't have to all the time. My head office is here. But my home in Peru I consider my main residence,' he said smoothly. 'I think you will like it there.' And he had the gall to smile.

Not if she could help it, she thought. And she did not trust his sudden change of tone or his sensuous smile, and she recognized the darkening gleam in his eyes. Abruptly she got to her feet. 'With you there I doubt that, and I have had enough to eat,' she said curtly. 'I am going to bed…alone,' she added and turned to walk out of the room.

She had almost made it when a strong arm grabbed her around the waist.

She tried to move but his arm was like a steel band around her, and she was suddenly terribly conscious of his hard thighs against her own, and she laid a restraining hand on his broad chest.

'You are angry I brought you to New York. I understand that, Emily. But be aware my patience is not limitless.' His other hand reached up and tangled in her hair and his dark head descended, claiming her mouth with his own.

'Remember that later,' he husked when she was breathless in his arms.

She looked up into his dark, smouldering eyes, her heart racing, and she swayed slightly, then stiffened.

For heaven's sake, woman, she derided herself. The man kidnapped you, stuck you in New York—what kind of weak-willed idiot are you? And she pushed out of his arms.

CHAPTER NINE

SHE woke up alone in the big bed, only the indentation on the pillow reminding her Anton had shared it with her for the second night running without touching her. Emily told herself she was glad. She had been asleep when he had joined her the first night and she had turned her back on him when he had slid into bed last night and his mocking comment still echoed in her head.

'I often wondered what the cold shoulder meant, and now I know.' And two minutes later the even sound of his breathing had told her he was asleep.

But then yesterday morning with Anton had been a disaster, and the rest of the day not a lot better...

Like a general leading his troops, he whisked her around Manhattan. Bought her a cell phone and programmed it for her with all the numbers he thought she needed. Then he bought her a mountain of clothes, overriding all her objections. As his wife she had a position to uphold and the few clothes she had with her were not enough. Which was hardly her fault.

By the time the limousine stopped outside his office at one in the afternoon, they were barely speaking. She refused his offer to accompany him inside. Instead she had the chauffeur drive her around the main attractions. On returning to the apartment she was surprised when Maria told her her computer had arrived, and been set up in one of the spare bedrooms for her exclusive use.

She stared in disbelief at the bedroom. A computer was on an obviously new desk, a black leather chair positioned in front and the walls were lined with bookshelves—a perfect study, in fact.

She spun around on the new chair a few times, then started to work. She quickly began answering a backlog of e-mails.

One lifted her spirits no end. A confirmation that the expedition she had been researching for the last few months was definitely going ahead. All the licences and permissions had been obtained from the Venezuelan government. The expedition was to find a pirate ship sunk off the Las Rocas archipelago. She was to join the research ship in Caracas on the twentieth of September, as the onboard marine archaeologist to map out in detailed scale drawings any finds they might make on the seabed. Hopefully they would find signs of the ship and the cargo, which was reliably reported in ancient documents to include gold and treasure from all over Europe.

Hunched over the computer, she laughed out loud as she read the reply to her acceptance. Jake Hardington was a world-renowned highly successful treasure hunter and a great flirt, though Emily knew he was an extremely happy married man—his wife, Delia, was a friend of hers.

'Something has made you happy.'

She jerked her head up in surprise at the sound of Anton's voice. 'Where did you come from?'

Six feet four of arrogant male was standing looking down at her, dressed in an immaculately tailored business suit, but to her dismay the instant picture in her mind's eye was of the same body naked. His dark gaze met hers, and she fought back a blush at the thought.

'Work,' he drawled sardonically. 'And I guess I am not the cause of your good humour.'

'No. Yes…' she garbled her response. Because half the reason for the embarrassing colour tingeing her cheeks was guilt. She had no intention of telling Anton her news. His derogatory statements about her career, and the very fact she was here instead of in London, were enough to keep her lips sealed.

'I mean I was delighted.' She retrieved the moment. 'You bought me a computer and everything. Thank you.'

He bent over her and brushed a strand of hair from her brow, and ran his fingers down her cheek and around her throat to tip her head back. Nervously she licked her lips as his hooded eyes ran slowly over her, and inwardly she trembled.

'Anything you want you can have, you do know that,' he said huskily.

His mouth came down to cover hers, and as his tongue stroked against hers a familiar heat ignited deep inside her.

'Is now pay-back time?' she muttered resentfully as she remembered where she was and why, and abruptly Anton straightened.

'You disappoint me, Emily. I have never paid for a woman and you demean yourself by trying to play the whore, when we both know you are the opposite,' he said, his cold hard eyes looking down at her—in more ways than one. 'Why let resentment cloud your judgement?' He shook his dark head. 'Why deprive your body of what you so obviously want?' His dark gaze lowered to where her nipples pressed taut against the soft cotton of her top. 'You're a stubborn woman, Emily, but no match for me,' he warned and, turning on his heel, he left the room.

Inexplicably Emily had felt about two inches tall…

* * *

Thinking about it now made her grimace. Still, this morning was a new day, she told herself, a free day, and leapt out of bed. Quickly she showered and dressed in navy linen trousers and a brief self-supporting white top; she popped her cell phone in her trousers pocket for easy access in case she saw something she wanted to photograph, slung her bag over her shoulder and ventured out again into the city, a gleam of mischief in her blue eyes.

Anton was not going to have it all his own way. She dismissed the chauffeured limousine, insisting she was only going for a walk, and sauntered along the street.

At the first subway station she dashed down the stairs and squeezed on board a train that was just leaving the platform. She watched as the doors shut, and saw a look of shock on the face of a young man as he lifted a cell phone to his ear. She leapt off at the next station and dashed across the platform and jumped onto another one. She stayed for two stops, then exited the train and walked back up to the street.

She had no idea where she was and she did not care. She was free…

The street was crowded, someone bumped into her and she laughed. It was great to be one of the masses again.

Anton surveyed the six men around the boardroom table. It had taken months to get this meeting arranged and if they all agreed it was going to be one of the biggest deals Wall Street had ever seen. He was sure they would. Sitting back in his chair, he let the Texan hold the floor—the man had been his guest on his yacht and they had already worked out how to present the deal.

He felt a vibration on his chest. Damn his cell phone. He pulled it from his pocket and glanced at the screen. Then leapt to his feet.

'Sorry, I am going to have to postpone this meeting.' Angry—he was furious by the time they had all left.

He lifted his cell phone to his ear. 'What the hell happened, Max? How could you possibly lose her?' He listened, then responded with a few choice words and strict instructions to find her immediately.

Emily glanced around. The skyscrapers she had thought so great after six hours of jumping on and off underground trains and walking around now seemed threatening. She had realized when she had sat down in a restaurant for lunch, whoever had bumped into her had stolen her cell phone. But it had not bothered her because she had still had her purse and money. Except now she wanted to flag a taxi home, she had suddenly realized she had no idea of her address…except overlooking Central Park…

She did anyway, but the taxi driver didn't appear to speak very good English. She got the impression Central Park was huge and she thought he asked if she was east or west. But looking at his swarthy features half hidden by a beard and the speculative gleam in his eyes he could have said *easy* and *western*. Not wanting to risk it, she looked for a public telephone. The only one she found had been vandalized and as a last resort she walked into a nearby police station.

The policeman on the desk looked at her as if she was crazy when she explained that her cell phone had been stolen with all her contact numbers in it, and she did not know her address, and the trouble she had with trying to get a taxi. Then she finally asked if she could use their telephone to call her husband and reluctantly gave him Anton's name as she did not know his number.

He made a call and then was perfectly charming, offering her a seat and coffee. Gratefully she took the cup and gave him a brilliant smile. American policemen were really great, she thought, sipping her coffee and leaning back in the surprisingly comfortable chair he had found for her. But inside her stomach was churning. Anton would be furious. He would probably send Max for her and Max certainly would not be very happy either, she realized rather belatedly.

The door opened and the hairs on the back of her neck prickled. Slowly she looked up, her gaze riveted on the man who stood silhouetted against the opening. With the light behind him she was not able to see his face clearly, which was maybe just as well. It was Anton and her heart missed a beat; the waves of rage coming off his big tense body were intimidating enough.

He strode past her and up to the desk. 'Thank you, officer, that is indeed my wife. I will take her off your hands now. Sorry for the inconvenience.'

Emily rose to her feet. 'Hello, Anton, I didn't…' She looked at him and the words froze in her throat. His black eyes returned her look with a glittering remorseless intensity that sent a shiver down her spine. Her legs threatened to cave in beneath her, and when he wrapped his big hand around her upper arm, rather than protest, she needed the support.

'Thank you, Grant,' she threw over her shoulder at the policeman as Anton marched her out of the door.

'"Thank you, Grant."' He mimicked derisively as he shoved her into the seat of a big black Ferrari parked in a no-parking zone, and slid in beside her.

He gunned the engine and never spoke a word until they were back in the apartment.

She turned to glance warily up at him. 'I'm sorry I got lost.'

Anton stood towering over her, his eyes scathingly raking her feminine form with a blatant sexual thoroughness that brought a blush to her cheeks.

Emily could feel the unwanted flush of awareness flooding through her body at his insulting scrutiny. He looked dynamic and supremely masculine in his light grey suit jacket taut over his broad shoulders, his white shirt open at the neck, his tie hanging loose, and helplessness engulfed her as she stared at him.

Anton's grim voice broke the lengthening silence. 'You are lucky you only got lost. The desk sergeant told me about the taxi driver.' He cast her a hard, contemptuous look. 'Rather than wasting your time and talent trying to dodge Security and almost getting raped… Why don't you grow up? When are you going to get it in your damn-fool head you are no longer a foot-loose girl? Diving thirty feet off yachts and heaven knows what else. You are my wife, you are under my protection and yet you deliberately put yourself and those around you at risk. Two men lost their jobs today because of your actions, and I have probably lost the biggest deal ever as I had to walk out halfway through a meeting to find you. I hope you are proud of yourself.'

If Anton had shouted and raged at her as she had expected she could have handled it, but his contemptuous condemnation of her behaviour brought home to her how stupidly reckless she had been.

'No,' she said simply. 'I never meant anybody to lose their job. Please don't fire them.'

One dark brow arched sardonically. 'I won't…if I have your word you will stop this rebellious behaviour and start behaving as a wife should.'

'You mean bow and scrape to you,' she flared.

'Cut out the dramatics, Emily,' Anton responded and finally touched her, his hands closing over her shoulders. 'You know what I mean,' he grated, his hand sliding down her back to cup her buttocks and pull her hard against his thighs, and she trembled as the evidence of his masculine arousal pressed against her stomach.

'But, so help me God, Emily—' his black eyes burned down into hers '—if you ever put me through that again, I will lock you up and throw away the key.' She gasped, and his mouth crashed down on hers, his tongue thrusting desperately between her parted lips, passionately demanding.

She should fight, she knew she should because there was no love involved and for a million other reasons. But two long days of frustration were having a debilitating effect on her ability to resist him. Then why should she? The impish question slid into her brain.

Anton was satisfied with lust, he wanted nothing more, and, if she was honest, she finally admitted she no longer had the will or the conviction to fight the sexual attraction she felt for him. There was no point in pretending it was love even to herself…

She looped her arms around his neck, and felt his great body shudder and realized he really had been worried about her. It gave her a fuzzy feeling inside, and, though she was loath to admit, hope for the future. She ran her fingers through his thick black hair, and held him closer, responding with a hunger that matched his own. Later in bed two nights of abstinence took a long time to satisfy.

The next morning when she walked in the kitchen Max was seated at the table, waiting for her. 'Max, I might have guessed. Anton told you.' And pulling out a chair, she sat down opposite him, and poured herself a cup of coffee. Of Maria there was no sign.

'He didn't have to tell me. My operative informed me the minute you got on the subway yesterday. You do realize, Emily, it was not skill, but blind luck you caught that train and lost him. And sheer bloody luck—' he swore '—that you were not mugged, raped or worse…'

'You are forgetting kidnapped,' she said facetiously and

smiled. She had not forgotten the reason she was here instead of London.

'You think that is funny?' he snapped. 'Well, let me tell you, Emily, I have had to tell a couple in the past that their child was found dead after having been buried alive for three days in a hole in the ground, and it is not funny.'

'Sorry.' Emily instantly sobered. Max probably did not know Anton had tricked her into coming to New York.

'So you should be. What the hell are you trying to do to Anton?' She had never seen Max so coldly angry. 'I thought when he met and married you, it was the best thing that ever happened to him. At last he had love in his life, something he has never had before, but now I am not so sure. What on earth were you playing at?' He eyed her contemptuously. 'I have never in all the years I have known him seen him so distraught. He is a wealthy, powerful man and as such has enemies, and you are his wife, and should be aware of the danger. He damn near had a heart attack yesterday when you disappeared. He is by nature a loner, a very private man, not to mention a worka-holic. But yesterday he dropped everything to call out the police, anyone and everyone, even the press to try and find you. The man worships the ground you walk on, and you repay him with a childish trick. Well, not any more. One of my top opera-tives will be arriving any minute now, and I want your word you will not try to give her the slip...understood? The alterna-tive is I stick to you as well.'

Reeling under the verbal tongue-bashing, and amazed Max actually thought Anton adored her and was distraught she had gone missing, Emily meekly agreed.

Mercedes arrived moments later. She was a little older than Emily, and after half an hour of conversation over coffee Emily liked her. She had a wealth of experience of life in New York and a great sense of humour. From that day on she arrived every morning and accompanied Emily on visits to museums, art galleries. She showed her the best places to shop—not that Emily found herself actually enjoying her time in New York.

On a Friday night two weeks later Emily stood in front of the mirror and hardly recognized herself. Her blonde hair was swept up in an intricate twist. The black dress was strapless and clung to her every curve, one of Anton's purchases, as was the diamond necklace she fastened around her throat. He had arrived back from the office ten minutes ago and dropped the necklace he had first given her on the yacht on the dresser as he headed for the bathroom shedding his clothes, with instructions that she wear it tonight.

Their relationship had developed since Emily had got lost. She had quit sniping at him, and begun to accept his perception of marriage, and it seemed to work. The sex was great and, if sometimes she wished for the love she had dreamt of, she told herself no one could have everything. But what she had with Anton came close.

She had spent the last two weeks exploring New York with Mercedes when she was not sitting at her computer working. Which was just as well, because apart from a few social dinner engagements Anton said they were obliged to attend, she did not see a lot of him.

Max was right about him; he was a workaholic. He left for the office at six in the morning and rarely returned before eight, they dined and went to bed and the passion between them flared as white-hot as ever.

Civil and sex was easy under the circumstances and she could understand why it appealed to Anton. He had no time for anything else…

The only reason he had returned by seven tonight was because they were attending the opening of an exhibition of Peruvian art, as guests of the Peruvian ambassador to the USA, and they had thirty minutes to get there.

She heard the shower switch off, and, with one last look at her reflection, walked out of the bedroom and into the lounge. She stood looking out of the huge window, wondering how her life had come to this, waiting for Anton...

'The necklace looks good.' She turned. Anton, wearing a dark evening suit and snowy white pleated shirt, was standing a few feet away.

'How did—?'

'The reflection in the glass.' He read her mind.

He looked strikingly attractive and it wasn't just the suit. Tall and brutally handsome, he exuded an aura of strength and power and tightly leashed sexuality that took her breath away.

'We should leave; we are going to be late,' Emily said coolly. And he nodded his dark head in agreement and took her arm.

Slowly it had dawned on Emily that outside the bedroom Anton had an air of detachment about him that rather confirmed Max's comment that he was a loner. And the longer they stayed in New York, the more she began to accept that this was the real Anton. Not the deceitful seducer or the fun-loving companion he had been on the island. But the one hundred per cent seriously focused international tycoon. His work was his life; everything else was peripheral.

In a way it made life easier, she thought as they entered the Prestige's art gallery half an hour later.

Anton was a man with little or no emotion; even his revenge had lost its flavour for him, after he had revealed it to her. She remembered his dismissal of it with why spoil their marriage as the two people concerned were dead. She should have realized then… The death of his mother was probably the only event that had touched his heart in any way. Everything else was business.

'Emily. You seem miles away.'

She cast him a sidelong glance and a smile. 'No, I'm fine.' She glanced around the vast room. The walls were hung with paintings, sculptures stood on podiums, and a grand staircase led to another level and more paintings. All New York's élite seemed to be present. Waiters with loaded trays of champagne moved smoothly through the crowd, others with loaded trays of canapés circled non-stop. 'This looks very nice.'

'Damned with faint praise,' Anton murmured against her ear. And then she was being introduced to the Peruvian ambassador and his wife, and his beautiful daughter Lucita.

She was small and voluptuous with huge sultry eyes. She gave Emily a saccharine smile before turning to gush all over Anton.

Not another one… Emily thought, and found herself standing alone as Lucita wrapped her arms around Anton's neck and made to kiss him. He subtly averted his head so she caught his cheek instead of his mouth. But Emily knew… She saw it in the spiteful glance Lucita gave her, when Anton caught her shoulders and put her back at arm's length.

'So you are his wife. We were all surprised when we heard Anton had married. Have you known each other long?'

Emily opened her mouth to reply, but Anton's arm slipped around her waist and he pulled her lightly against him and answered for her.

'Long enough to know Emily was the only woman for me.'

Congratulations were offered, but Emily could sense the underlining hostility. She glanced up at Anton and caught the savage satisfaction in his expression as he smiled and they moved on.

'What was that all about?' she demanded. 'I thought the ambassador was a friend of yours.'

Something moved in the dark depths of his eyes. 'Not really. I have very few friends—plenty of business acquaintances, though,' he said, leading her slowly towards a wall to view the artwork. 'As for the ambassador, he has to appear to be my friend or lose his job, and that is what gets his goat,' he drawled mockingly.

'Are you really that powerful?' she asked.

'Yes.' One word and he took two glasses of champagne from a passing waiter and handed her one and slipped his arm around her again.

For a moment Emily looked at him. 'Is that all?'

'I sponsored the exhibition, and I also sponsor the artists.' He gestured with his glass to a huge abstract painting, all red, green and black. 'What do you think of that?'

'I'm amazed.'

'You like it?' His dark brows rose quizzically.

'No, I hate it,' she answered honestly. 'But I'm amazed you sponsored the event and the artists. I wouldn't have thought you had time.'

Anton chuckled, a low husky sound, his arm tightening around her. 'Your honest opinion is charming, though I doubt the artist would appreciate it. As for my sponsoring the event, it does not take time, just rather a lot of money.'

'I'm impressed all the same,' Emily declared as he propelled her further around the room. 'I am also hungry,' she murmured and took a canapé from a passing waiter and popped it in her mouth.

At just that moment someone spoke to Anton, she swallowed the food, and was introduced to an eminent banker and his wife.

For the next hour they circled the gallery. Anton was greeted by a host of people, and Emily shook hands and smiled in between sipping champagne and popping canapés in her mouth.

As for the paintings, two she really liked. A somewhat abstract landscape of the Andes with mist swirling that looked almost mystical, and a small painting of a little Indian boy squatting on the ground and laughing, with what was obviously his father's big black hat on his head.

Anton bought both.

'You didn't have to do that.'

'I wanted to.' He pulled her close and led her through the crowd towards the exit. 'And if I had given you the choice we would never get out of here—women take a notoriously long time to make a decision, and we are going to dinner. I am hungry.'

Emily gave him a dazzling smile. 'Anton, that is a terrible chauvinistic comment, even for you.'

'So? I want you...out of here.' His dark eyes held hers and she was captivated by the amusement, the sensual warmth in the inky depths. For a second she was back on his Greek island, and her pulse began to race, and anticipation shivered through her. Was he aware of it?

'We're leaving,' he rasped and she knew he was as they made for the exit.

'Going?' Lucita with three friends stopped them as they reached the foyer.

'Why don't you join us, Anton? We are going on to a supper club.' She spoke solely to Anton, ignoring Emily.

'No, Lucita,' he said in a voice that held an edge of steel. 'I have better things to do,' and with that parting shot he urged Emily outside.

But the moment was broken for Emily. 'That was a bit brutal—you obviously know the lady very well,' she said, moving out of his protective arm. 'And I saw the look on your face when you spoke to the ambassador, and it wasn't very edifying.'

'Edifying?' He raised an eyebrow. 'You are *so* English, Emily.'

He ushered her into the back seat of the limousine without saying another word, and slid in beside her. He closed the glass partition, and then turned to look at her.

'Yes, I know Lucita well, but not as well as you imagine. I knew her brother a lot better.' His face, shadowed in the dim light, was hard. 'Do you want to know the truth, or do you want to mark her down as another woman I have slept with? You seem to be under the impression I have slept with hundreds, which I have not. I would not even make double figures, but my reputation goes against me. Something you could not begin to understand, given the charmed life you have led.'

'I wouldn't say—'

'Say nothing and listen for a change. I was twelve when my mother brought me back to Peru to live with my grandmother. At first I went to the local school, but at fourteen I was sent to the best boarding school in the country, and that is where I met Lucita's brother. We became friends, because he was bullied unmercifully by the other boys and I stood up for him. Unfortunately for Pedro, he took after his mother, who, you might have noticed, is a small, quiet lady who I have great respect and sympathy for, but she is and always has been completely under her husband's thumb.

'Pedro and I studied together; we visited each other's home in the holidays, and played football, badly.' He grimaced. 'He had an artistic soul, and for two years we were friends, Lucita as well, until his father discovered my parentage. They were forbidden to see me again. And the man did his damnedest to get me thrown out of school.'

'Oh, Anton….' She couldn't imagine how he must have felt. He had made light of his parentage, but now she realized for a young boy it must have been hard.

'Don't worry. He was a minor government official at the time and he did not succeed. But he ruined his son's life, he sent him to another school, where apparently he was bullied again, and twelve months later Pedro committed suicide. I stood in the background at his funeral, the only teenage friend there.'

No wonder Anton had been distraught discovering his sister had committed suicide; his childhood friend had done the same.

'So you see why it gives me great satisfaction to watch the man having to be polite to me now, and I am not going to apologize for that. As for his daughter, she is just like him— the only difference is she would have me in a heartbeat simply because I am wealthy.'

'I'm sorry. I had no idea.'

He sat back in the seat. 'I told you the first time we met. I just knew you would feel sorry for me, and your sympathy is misplaced. You're too naive for your own good, Emily.' But the indulgent smile he gave her took the sting out of his words.

'I might be naive...' she looked at him curiously, a sudden thought occurring to her '...but answer me this. Why didn't you marry Lucita to get back at her father? Rather than waiting to marry me to get back at mine?'

He stilled. 'The idea never entered my head.' He shook his head, his dark eyes widening on her, and then he burst out laughing. 'Oh, Emily, I might have a vengeful streak, but I am not a masochist. You are delightful and drop-dead gorgeous and Lucita is an evil witch in comparison.'

Emily stared at him in shock. Was that a compliment? She did not know what to think...and, taking full advantage, Anton leant forward and kissed her.

The limousine stopped and Anton helped her out. 'I thought we were going to eat out,' she said as he led her into their apartment.

He smiled a soft, slow curl of his firm lips, and moved his hand from her arm to snake around her shoulders, staring into her eyes from mere inches away. 'I am still hungry, *niña*,' he said softly, his slight accent more pronounced than usual, 'but the food can wait till later.' His dark eyes smouldered as he held her and he bent closer and she felt the hard warmth of his mouth brush against her parted lips.

Far into the night Emily made love with Anton with a long, slow tenderness, a passion that brought tears to her eyes because she knew to Anton it was still just sex...

CHAPTER TEN

ANTON snapped shut his laptop, and fastened his seat belt.

They would be landing in ten minutes, and it could not be too soon. He had clinched a major deal and cleared his work schedule for the next month.

He had not seen Emily in weeks, it was becoming ridiculous and he was determined to do something about the situation. A frown crossed his broad brow. They had been married three months, the sex was great and he should be satisfied. Yet the amount of time they had spent with each other was limited.

After three weeks in New York they had returned to London. Emily had caught up with her research. But he had been obliged to travel to the Middle East. In July they had returned to Greece, but he had taken frequent trips to Athens and Moscow.

The beginning of August Emily was supposed to have accompanied him to Australia. But Helen had given birth to a baby boy and Emily had gone back to England to help look after the mother and Anton could hardly object.

But after almost two weeks on his own he had called her last night and told her to be packed—they were going to Peru tomorrow. Which gave him time to kiss the baby's head and leave. It was time they had a baby of their own; in fact Emily might already be pregnant. Not that she had said anything during their telephone calls, but then she never said much anyway...

A frustrating hour later, after discovering she was not at their apartment, he stopped the Bentley outside the Fairfax home in Kensington.

Mindy, the housekeeper, showed him into the drawing room.

Emily was sitting on a low chair, the rays of the afternoon sun shining through the window casting a golden halo around her head, and in her arms she held a baby.

She was totally oblivious of his arrival, her whole attention on the tiny infant, her beautiful face wreathed in smiles. 'You are a beautiful little boy.' She chuckled. 'Yes—yes, you are, and your aunty Emily loves you.' And as he watched she kissed the baby's cheek.

He choked...and felt an unfamiliar stab of something like emotion in the region of his heart. 'Emily.' She turned her head to look at him.

'Anton, I never heard you arrive.' Slowly rising to her feet, cradling the baby, she walked across to him. 'Look, isn't he gorgeous?'

She was gorgeous. Her hair was parted in the middle and tucked behind her delicate ears to fall in a silken mass down her back. She was wearing blue jeans that clung to her slim hips and long legs, and a soft white sweater.

He looked at the child. The baby was snuggled against her breast, and he wished it were him...

'Yes, wonderful.' He reached a finger to touch the baby's cheek.

'Helen and Tom have decided to call him Charles after our father.'

Anton looked down into her blue eyes and saw the flash of defiance she made no attempt to hide, and his mouth tightened. She was an exquisitely beautiful but wilful woman and she was never going to accept the truth about her father. As for him, he didn't care any more…

'A solid name. I like it,' he said smoothly.

'Charles Thomas.' Helen, coming in, moved to take the child from Emily's arms. 'Anton, good to see you—now, would you mind taking your wife back home, before she takes over my baby completely, and try making one of your own?' She laughed.

They all laughed but he noticed Emily avoided his gaze.

'I intend to do just that.' Anton reached for Emily and drew her into his arms, his dark eyes searching her guarded blue. 'This is a brief visit, Helen,' he said without taking his eyes off his wife. 'We are flying out to my place in Peru tomorrow.'

Just seeing Anton walk in the door had made Emily's heart lurch. It had taken all her self-control to walk slowly towards him and show him the baby, and now, held in his arms, she felt a bittersweet longing shudder through her. When he kissed her the warmth of his lips, the scent of him, aroused her in a second.

'We are leaving.' Anton lifted his head and she looked up into his dark eyes, and saw the promise of passion, and knew hers showed the same.

'Get out of here, you two,' Helen said with a chuckle. 'You're embarrassing the baby.'

As soon as they entered the penthouse Anton slid an arm around Emily's waist and pulled her towards him.

'I have waited two long weeks for this,' he husked.

'Why? Were there no willing women in Australia?' And Emily was only half teasing. She knew in her heart of hearts she loved him, yet she could not let herself trust him, and the green-eyed monster haunted her thoughts when he was gone. Not something she was proud of.

'Plenty willing but none that looked like you.' His brilliant eyes gleamed as he bent his head and covered her mouth with his.

So he had been looking, was Emily's last thought as, helplessly, her eyelids fluttered down and she raised her slender arms to wrap around his broad shoulders, her body arching into his.

His kiss possessive, his tongue traced the roof of her mouth and curled with hers, and her blood flowed like liquid heat through her veins. His hand slipped up beneath her sweater and trailed up her spine, making her shudder as he opened her bra. Then his hand stroked around to slip up beneath the front of her sweater to find the thrusting swell of her breasts.

'You are wearing far too many clothes,' he rasped, and suddenly she was swept up into his arms, his mouth desperately claiming hers again as, with more haste than finesse, he carried her to the bedroom and dropped her on the bed. 'Get them off.'

Her eyes opened and her gaze fixed on Anton ripping off his clothes like a man possessed. Naked, he was masculine perfection. Tall and broad, his muscular chest rising not quite steadily and his lean hips and thighs cradling the virile power of his fully aroused sex.

'You want me to do it for you.' He chuckled, a deep sexy sound that vibrated across her nerve endings, and, leaning over her, he stripped her jeans and briefs from her legs, before just as efficiently dispensing with her sweater and bra.

His hands cupped her naked breasts and her nipples hardened beneath his skilful touch.

'Missed me…?' He looked deep into her eyes, and she could not lie.

'Yes,' she sighed and reached for him. But inside her heart cried for what might have been. She could have been the happiest woman alive, a loving wife, but Anton had destroyed that dream with his revelation about his real motivation for marrying her.

The really soul-destroying part was that Anton didn't even see it. He was perfectly content so long as the sex was good.

Angry with herself for loving him, she reared up and, pushing him down, straddled his thighs, determined to drive him mad with desire. Why should she be the only one?

'You are eager—maybe I should stay away more often,' he said with a husky amusement in his tone, his great body stretched hard beneath her.

'Maybe you should.' She stared down into his brutally handsome face. He was watching her, a sensual gleam in his night-black eyes. He reached out a hand and captured her breast, his long fingers tweaking a pouting nipple. She jerked back, heat flooding from her breast to her thighs, but she would not be deterred from her mission to make him squirm for a change. She wrapped her fingers around his aroused manhood and lowered her head, her long hair brushing the length of his torso, and tasted him.

His great body bucked and she heard him groan, she felt his tension, and she shook with the effort it took to control her own heightened desire for him. She continued until he was straining for release, then stopped.

She raised her head. His eyes were smouldering like the depths of hell, his face taut, and she closed her fingers gently around him.

'Not yet,' she murmured. Running her tongue around her full lips, she saw the fiery passion burn brighter in his eyes. Deliberately she leant forward and trailed a row of kisses from his belly up the centre of his chest, straying once to tongue a small male nipple before moving on to finally cover his mouth with her own, her hand stroking lower to cup the essence of the man. Suddenly he was lifting her, impaling her on his fiercely erect manhood.

Wild and wanton, she rode him, his body arching up as he filled her to the hilt with increasingly powerful thrusts. His hands gripped her waist, making her move, twisting, turning her where he desired, as they duelled for sexual supremacy. She cried out at the tug of his mouth on her rigid nipples, and arched back, fighting for control.

Emily succumbed first, convulsing around him. She was mindless in her ecstasy, clenching him with every spasm in a ferociously prolonged orgasm. She heard him cry her name and his body shuddered as he joined her in a climax that finally stopped her breath. The little death.

Some time later she opened her eyes to find Anton staring down at her. 'That was some welcome home, Emily,' he said, curving her into the side of his body. She brushed a few tendrils of damp hair from her face, smoothing the long length over one shoulder and down to her breast, where his hand lingered.

'Yes, well…' It was what he expected, she thought, suddenly feeling cold inside. 'Two weeks without sex is not good for anyone,' she threw out. And saw a flicker of some emotion she could not put a name to in the depths of his dark eyes.

'Tell me about it,' he said dryly, and then added, 'It must be tough for Helen—no sex for a few weeks after the birth, I believe.'

'I doubt if Helen minds. She has a beautiful little boy to love.'

'And would you mind, if you were pregnant? You could be.'

The question blind-sided her. No, she couldn't, but, seeing Helen with her baby for the last two weeks, it had brought home to her how much she would have loved to have Anton's child if only he had loved her… But there was no future in thinking like that. Anton did not believe in love and was therefore incapable of loving anyone; he had told her so quite emphatically.

Whereas she had been a trusting soul all her life and Anton had destroyed that part of her nature with a few words, and if he ever found out she loved him it would destroy her completely; all she had left was her pride.

'I have never thought about it, and I am not in any hurry to find out,' she lied and moved along the bed, away from the warmth of his big body.

He caught her chin between his finger and thumb and turned her head back so she had no choice but to look at him. 'Seeing you with the baby today I realized you are a natural, Emily. You will make a wonderful mother.'

A tender, caring Anton was the last thing she needed. She felt guilty enough as it was, though she had no need to be. He had deceived her into marrying him; her deceit was nothing in comparison.

'Maybe.' She shook her head, dislodging his hand, and tried a smile but suddenly a thought hit her... And, jumping off the bed in a show of bravado, she stood up totally naked and stared down at him. 'But we have only been married a few months, and, let's face it, we hardly have a marriage made in heaven. A bit of time to adjust to each other before having to adjust to a baby is no bad thing,' she offered and, turning, she walked quickly into the bathroom. She had just remembered she hadn't taken her pill the last two nights, because she had spent the weekend with Tom and Helen...

She snagged a large towel from the rail and tucked it around her body sarong-style. Then found the packet in the back of the bathroom cabinet where she had carelessly left it while Anton was away.

She took two out... Was it dangerous to take two? She had a feeling it was. She scanned the packet, but it didn't say. She placed the packet on the back of the vanity unit and popped one pill in her mouth and dropped one in the basin. Then, filling a glass with water, she swallowed it down, and let the water run to wash away the other.

'Headache?' She heard his voice and spun around to see Anton naked and leaning against the bathroom door. 'So soon?'

'Kind of,' she murmured.

Something predatory and ruthless glinted in his dark eyes as he strolled towards her and reached over the basin to where the packet lay and picked it up. 'A contraceptive pill that doubles as a headache cure. How convenient.' She saw the banked-down anger in his black eyes and was afraid.

A naked man should not be able to look threatening, she thought distractedly, but Anton did. As though sensing her thoughts, he grabbed a towel and wrapped it around his hips.

'What—no response, Emily?' he drawled, closing in on her, and she took a few steps back until she met the wall. 'No excuse, you devious little bitch?'

She sucked in a furious breath. 'That is rich coming from you,' she threw at him, her eyes flashing. He was not going to intimidate her, and she would not allow it. 'As for an excuse, I don't need one. Yes, I am on the pill—so what?' she challenged him, her anger laced with scorn. 'My body is my own—you borrow it for sex. Nothing more and, may I point out—' and she poked him in the chest with her finger '—it was your own idea; love does not come into the equation.'

Emily was on a roll and could not stop. She didn't notice the sudden narrowing of his eyes or the tension in his great body. She was too overcome with emotion—something he knew nothing about. 'Do you honestly think I would bring a baby into the world without love, just to fulfil some dynastic craving of yours? You must be joking.'

For over three months she had fought to keep control of her

emotions around Anton, but now her composure was beginning to shatter.

'Nothing to say?' she demanded into the lengthening silence, and dragged an angry if slightly unsteady breath into her suddenly oxygen-starved lungs. 'Why am I not surprised? You are so damned sure of yourself, with your limitless wealth and arrogance, it is probably the first time in years you have found something you can't buy…a baby.'

She shook her head despairingly. Was it possible to love and hate someone at the same time? she wondered. Because right at this moment, with Anton standing half naked, bristling with rage, her stupid heart still ached for him, and yet her head hated him. She tried to walk past him. What was the point in arguing?

Anton had kept control on his temper by a thread and now it broke. Ice-cold fury glittered in his eyes as he looked at her. 'That's right. I bought you,' he stated coldly. 'And nobody does me out of a deal. Certainly not you, my wilful little wife.'

He wanted to tear her limb from limb as she stood there, her long hair falling around her shoulders in golden disarray, the expression on her beautiful face one of contempt. Yet she had been deceiving him for weeks, possibly months.

'How long—how long have you been taking the pill?' he demanded, and, grasping a handful of her hair, he twisted it around his wrist and pulled her head back, the better to look into her deceitful eyes.

'Since the week after we met,' Emily shot back and told him the truth. 'When I was foolish enough to think you and I might have an affair. After all, that is what you are renowned for and that was all I expected.' She trembled at the rage in the depths of his eyes, but refused to back down. 'Imagine my surprise when you proposed marriage. And, idiot that I was, I accepted, labouring in the misguided notion that I loved you. But you soon put me right on that score, Anton. Lucky for me I already had the pills.'

Anton stared down into her blazing blue eyes fiercely battling the urge to cover her mouth with his and drive her hate-filled words down her throat. Emily had quite confidently expected to be his mistress, going so far as taking the pill in preparation. But he had surprised her with offering marriage. There was only one conclusion he could draw—she thought she was too good to have his child.

'Did you ever intend to tell me?' he demanded. 'Or was I to remain in ignorance for years?'

'Oh, I doubt it would be for more than two at the very most,' she drawled scathingly. 'You said yourself lust burns out and, for a man with your sexual appetite, I know I will not have to wait long before you are unfaithful, and then I can divorce you and you can't do a damn thing about it. Except pay up… But I'm not greedy, just enough to make sure Fairfax Engineering is totally free from you. Your one mistake was not asking me to sign a pre-nup. I would have done—I would have done anything you wanted until you revealed your real reason for marrying me. Well, you should be proud, Anton. You taught me well.' As Emily watched a shuttered expression came over his face, and his hand fell from her hair and he moved back from her.

'Too well, it would seem.' Reaching, he tugged the towel from her slender form. His rapier-like glance raked her from head to toe as though he had never seen her before, and she trembled.

'You are beautiful, but you have just proved you are a Fairfax just like your father, and now I find I would not have you as the mother of my child if you paid me,' he drawled derisively, and with a shrug he turned and strode out of the bathroom.

She watched him warily for a moment; there was a defeated look to the curve of his broad shoulders as he walked towards the bed. He ran a hand distractedly through his black hair, and then he straightened. Emily picked up the towel and wrapped it around her shivering body and took a hesitant step towards the open door, concerned. She must have made some sound because Anton spun around.

'No need to be wary. I am not going to jump you.' He smiled a bitter twist of his sensuous lips. 'The bedroom is yours, but be aware a divorce is not, unless I choose.'

She must have rocks in her head, worrying about him, Emily thought, advancing into the room.

A hand on her shoulder woke her from a restless sleep; she blinked and opened her eyes. And found Anton standing over her, dressed in a black shirt, black trousers and a black leather jacket, a mug of coffee in his hand. 'Drink this and hurry up and dress. You can have breakfast on board—we are leaving in less than an hour.'

She pulled the sheet over her breasts. 'Leaving…going where?' She was confused. 'I don't understand…I thought after last night…'

'That I would leave you? No, Emily, not yet. You are coming to Peru with me. I promised to prove to you what a stuck-up degenerate your father was. Unlike you, I keep my promises.'

She looked at him. His face was hard, his eyes cold and dead. He caught her shoulders and hauled her into a sitting position. 'After that you can go where the hell you like,' he said with icy finality in his tone.

For Emily the flight to Peru was horrendous. Twelve hours of Anton being scrupulously polite when the steward was around, and ignoring her the rest of the time. Unfortunately the atmosphere gave her plenty of time to think, and she didn't like her thoughts. She was in love with Anton, always was and always would be, and there was absolutely no future in it. Their marriage had ended the day after the wedding…

Even now Anton was still sticking to his ridiculous story about her father. Yet at one time he had told her to forget it as the people concerned were dead. Memories of the past few months flooded her mind. Their battles at the beginning, and then, after her disappearance in New York, the passionate way they made up and Max's certainty that Anton cared for her. The art gallery where she got a better understanding of why he was as he was… After that night, if she was honest, they had got along rather well. Anton had come back to London with her while she did her research. The next time in New York they had had a weekend in the Hamptons with a stockbroker and his wife and, apart from discussing business with their host one night, they had had a wonderful relaxing weekend.

She glanced at him. He was seated at the opposite side of the plane as far away from her as he could get, his dark head bent as he concentrated on the article he was reading in a financial magazine. He had shed his jacket and the dark sweater he wore stretched across his wide shoulders. As she watched he flicked a hand through his black hair, sweeping it from his broad brow. Something she had seen him do a hundred times when he was concentrating, which she found oddly endearing.

No, not endearing—she must not think like that. Their marriage was ending, and this was the last act. Only the formalities of a divorce lay ahead. She had no illusions left, and maybe that was no bad thing.

Anton had told her once to grow up…well, now she had.

Emily stared down fascinated as the helicopter transported them from the Lima airport to Anton's ranch high up into the Andes.

The fertile plains on the coast gave way to a rocky terrain and ever larger majestic hills and mountains, but with miles of jungle-like vegetation, and amazing half-hidden valleys.

The whirring blades slowed as the helicopter descended into one such huge valley. Her eyes widened at the sight of an enormous sprawling house with castellated turrets that seemed to cover half an acre, with smaller buildings, and a road surrounding it. The place was a village all on its own. Lush green paddocks and cultivated fields gave way to the natural rolling hills rising ever higher in the far distance.

'Is this it?' she asked, glancing at Anton as he removed his headphones.

'Welcome to Casa Diaz,' he said and, leaping out of the helicopter, he came around and took her hand and helped her down. He kept a hold of it as they ducked beneath the whirling blades and dropped it when they straightened up. A battered Jeep was waiting for them.

The driver, wearing a big sombrero and an even bigger smile, leapt out. 'Welcome, boss and Señora Diaz.' Sweeping off his sombrero, he bowed and ushered them into the Jeep. A moment later her suitcase was dropped in the back, and they were off.

The next half-hour was a blur to Emily. All the staff were lined up in the hall to meet her and Anton made the introductions, then requested the housekeeper serve them coffee.

Emily was intensely conscious of his hand on her bare arm, and the tension in his long body, as he led her through wide double doors set to one side of the massive marble staircase that dominated the huge hall and into a room that had to be at least forty feet long. She pulled her arm free and glanced around.

Her eyes widened in awe and for a while she forgot his icy, intimidating presence. A vaulted ceiling, heavy dark timbers, white walls, almost completely obliterated by paintings and artifacts. The place was like a museum, and she was fascinated. Spanish and Indian art and sculptures were displayed together, some really ancient, and very probably original.

She walked slowly around the room, lost to everything as she examined paintings, pictures and sepia snapshots of family with avid interest.

CHAPTER ELEVEN

THE HOUSEKEEPER arrived with a tray bearing coffee and delicate little cakes. 'Your favourite, señor.' She smiled and placed the tray on a beautifully carved antique occasional table, set between three large sofas.

'I had no idea your home was so old,' Emily finally said, turning to Anton as the housekeeper left.

He quirked an eyebrow as much as to say *So what*? but actually said, 'Sit down and pour the coffee.'

She bristled at the brisk command, but did as he said. Automatically she spooned sugar into his, black and sweet just how he liked it, and grimaced. She knew the little things about him, but not the big, she realized sadly, and never would now. She added milk to hers, and held his out to him as he sat down on the sofa adjacent to her.

'To answer your question—' he drained his coffee-cup, placed it back on the table '—the Diaz family has lived on this land since the first Sebastian Emanuel Diaz arrived in South America with the conquistadores,' he said flatly. Rising to his feet, he walked across the room to the fireplace.

'But you told me your grandmother was disowned,' she said, her eyes following him as he leant negligently against the ornate wood-carved mantelpiece. 'How did you get it back?' she asked, tearing her gaze from his impressive form. Then she realized the stupidity of her question. 'Stupid question—you probably made the owner an offer they could not refuse.' She raised her eyes to his and answered for him, sarcasm tingeing her tone. He was a ruthless devil. What Anton wanted Anton got, and it would suit his sense of justice to retrieve the family home.

'No, I did not.' His firm lips quirked in the ghost of a smile, a reminiscent gleam in the dark eyes that met hers. 'My grandmother did, thirty years after being thrown out by her father, and a few years after he died. By then her older brother had managed to bankrupt the family. My grandmother stepped in, bought the place, and spent many happy years here with her own mother. A beautiful but weak woman, and of the old school who obeyed her husband in everything, but she died happy with her daughter at her bedside. Then for the last ten years of my grandmother's life my mother and I lived here.'

'Your grandmother must have been an amazing woman,' Emily exclaimed. To go from the disowned daughter and owner of a brothel to a landowner again was an enormous leap.

'She was a true descendant of the original Diaz with all the courage that entailed,' Anton responded, one dark brow arching sardonically. 'Unfortunately my mother and sister, though kind, loving women, did not inherit her strength of character.'

'I never realized—' Emily began.

'You never realized that my family was a lot older than yours, even though it is the illegitimate side that flourished,' he drawled mockingly. 'But then life is full of little surprises.' Straightening up, he moved towards her.

She glanced up. He was towering over her, his face hard, his eyes as black as jet. In that moment she could see him as a conquistador, ruthless and cruel as they swept through South America centuries ago, and a shiver of fear snaked up her spine.

'Now is the time for your surprise. Come. What I wish to show you is in my study.

'Sit down.' He gestured to a deep buttoned leather Chesterfield, placed a few feet away from a massive leather-topped desk in the wood-panelled room. He then walked behind the desk, and, taking a key from his pocket, he opened one of the drawers and withdrew an envelope. He looked at it for a moment, and she felt the tension in the room, the tension in Anton as he walked back towards her.

'Read this.' He held out the battered envelope, a gleam of mocking triumph in his dark eyes. 'Then call me a liar if you dare.'

Reluctantly she took the envelope by one corner, avoiding touching his hand. The postmark was English. Slowly, with a hand that trembled, she withdrew the folded notepaper, and opened it. A gasp of surprise escaped her. The return address was their family home in Kensington. No, it could not be... Then she began to read.

Two minutes later Emily carefully folded the letter and placed it back in the envelope and rose gracefully to her feet. 'Very interesting,' she said and forced a smile to her stiff lips. 'But would you mind if I studied this in my room?' she asked. 'I am exhausted after all the travelling. We can discuss this at dinner.'

'Still in denial,' he mocked, but rang a bell fitted in the wall. 'It never ceases to amaze me the lengths that the female of the species will go to, to avoid facing an unpleasant truth,' he drawled cynically. 'But as you wish—dinner will be early, at seven, to accommodate your exhaustion!'

A maid arrived at his call to show Emily out of the room.

Anton watched them leave, a frown creasing his broad brow. Emily had surprised him. He had thought she would be devastated seeing the proof of her father's deceit, but instead she had smiled coolly and asked for time to study the letter. But then why was he surprised? Once he had regretted telling her about her father, but not any more. Once he had thought that was the only stumbling block to a long and successful marriage, but that was before last night when he had realized she never had any intention of being his wife or having his children. She would have been quite happy to be his mistress, but when it came to anything else she was just as big a snob as her father.

He had dealt with slurs on his upbringing all his life, and they did not bother him. But the least one expected from a wife was respect. He would be well rid of her. A wayward thought slid into his cool mind...

Why not keep her as a mistress until he tired of her luscious body? Let her earn the divorce she wanted on her back.

No, he immediately dismissed the notion because his pride would not let him. Bottom line, for all her innocence she had used him as nothing more than a stud. Nobody ever used Anton Diaz.

He left to check his horses—at least they were honest.

Emily followed the maid up the grand staircase along a wide corridor and into a lovely bedroom. Definitely feminine in white and with the occasional touch of pink. A lace coverlet with a pink satin trim running through it graced a four-poster bed delicately draped in white muslin, the tie-backs pink satin to match. Definitely not the master suite, Emily concluded, and, casually dropping the letter onto a frill-trimmed dressing table, she looked for her suitcase. A shower and change and dinner.

The last supper, she thought, and opened a wardrobe door to find her clothes had already been unpacked. Walking into the *en suite*, she glanced at the free-standing bath, but opted for a shower. She really was tired after a sleepless night, followed a long-haul flight almost halfway around the globe, followed by the helicopter flight and, although because of the time zone it was late afternoon, she had been awake for over thirty-six hours.

Stripping off the trousers and blouse she had travelled in plus her underwear, she stepped into the shower.

Emily looked at her reflection in the mirror. She had left her hair loose, simply tucked it behind her ears, but she had taken care with her make-up, subtly shading her eyelids to emphasize the blue of her eyes, with a light coating of mascara on her long lashes. Her full lips she coated in a rose gloss. And the slightest trace of blusher accentuated her cheekbones.

She needed all the help she could get. She was no actress, but she was not about to let Anton see how much leaving him was going to hurt her. She loved him, but she had too much character to live life on his terms, knowing it would eventually destroy her.

The dress she wore was a pale blue crêpe sheath with small sleeves and a square-cut neck that just revealed the upper curves of her breasts and ended a few inches above her knees. She slipped silver sandals on her feet, and fastened the diamond and sapphire locket around her neck and the matching bracelet on her wrist, but left off her engagement ring. Let Anton make of that what he will, she thought bitterly. He would anyway—but he was in for a rude awakening…

She walked down the staircase at five to seven, and stood at the bottom of the stairs looking around. She had no idea where the dining room was.

'Señora, this way—the master, he wait.' The housekeeper appeared and beckoned her to follow. Taking a deep breath, Emily entered the room. Anton was standing at the head of a long table set with the finest linen, china and crystal.

He was wearing a dark evening suit and looked every inch the Spanish grandee: arrogant, remote but devastatingly attractive. The breath caught in her throat. His dark head lifted, his black eyes roaming over her. She saw the moment he recognized her jewellery and watched him stiffen.

They were like two strangers staring at each other across a room.

Then for one tense moment their eyes fused. Emily imagined she saw a flicker of some emotion in his before his hooded lids lowered slightly, masking his expression, and he spoke.

'Emily, you look lovely as always. Please be seated,' he offered, and pulled out a chair.

She smoothed suddenly damp palms down her thighs as she walked towards him and sat down. She picked up a napkin and folded it on her lap—anything rather than look at him again, until she got her breathing under control.

The hour that followed was surreal.

The housekeeper served the food course after course, and Anton ate everything with obvious enjoyment. His conversation was icily polite, restricted to each dish and the ingredients involved, and the relative merits of the red and white wine that was served.

While Emily had a problem swallowing anything, and her replies were verging on the monosyllabic.

'Excellent meal,' he complimented the housekeeper as she served the coffee, smiled and left.

'You did not seem to eat much, Emily.' He straightened back in his chair and fixed her with black gimlet eyes. 'Something not to your liking or has something given you indigestion—or someone…like your father?'

The gloves were off with a vengeance, and actually Emily felt relieved. But before she could respond he continued.

'Not very pleasant, is it, when you find out someone you love deceived you, as I discovered last night. And you have discovered tonight.' It was then she saw the tightly leashed anger in his black eyes.

And what did he mean…someone he loved deceived him…? He had never loved her, and the only reason his nose was out of joint was because she was not the brood mare he had been hoping for.

'Not at all,' she said smoothly. She was not going to respond to his taunts. Cool, calm and collected—that was her strategy. 'In fact I am greatly relieved. I have read the letter you gave me, and, true, it is disgraceful, the sentiments expressed disgusting and totally unacceptable. Please accept I deeply regret what happened to your sister.' She was painstakingly polite. 'The poor girl must have been heartbroken.'

'Deeply regret?' he snarled. 'Is that all you have to say?'

'No.' Emily had given a lot of thought to the people and circumstances surrounding the letter after reading it and she was curious, and wanted to delve a little deeper. 'Tell me, Anton, did you see much of your father?'

'Not a lot, but what the hell has that got to do with anything?'

'Humour me. Did he treat your half-sister like his own child? Was he older than your mother?'

'No…and thirty years older.' He rattled off the answers.

'Then that might explain it.'

'Explain what—that your father seduced my sister? Don't even try to make excuses.'

'Okay, I won't.' She sat up straighter in her chair. 'My father never wrote that letter. You were wrong.' His face went dark with rage, the veins at his temples standing out so prominently she thought he was going to burst a blood vessel. 'But you were also right,' she got in quickly. 'The writing is that of my grandfather, Charles Fairfax, who had to be over fifty when he had an affair with your sister, which I suppose, in a way, makes it worse.'

Anton's black eyes flared in shocked disbelief. 'Your grandfather.'

She had been wrong, Emily thought, seeing the horror in his eyes. Anton was capable of emotion, but not one she envied him. 'Yes. My grandfather,' she said bluntly. 'An easy mistake to make,' she offered to soften the blow. 'Charles is a family name—the eldest son is always called Charles until my brother Thomas. Because my father was never on good terms with his own father so was never going to name his own son after him.'

'I cannot believe Suki…' Anton began and stopped.

He looked shell-shocked—a first for her arrogant husband, Emily was sure. 'It is true,' she continued. 'My father and aunt Lisa were horrified by the behaviour of their father when they were old enough to realize what he was really like. He was an out-and-out womanizer, a complete waster, the black sheep of the family. My grandfather and grandmother led completely separate lives but divorce was never an option. They shared the same house—you have seen my family home, it is more than big enough,' she said dryly. 'After he died when I was about seven, his name was never mentioned again. He was a horrible man and the whole family was disgusted by him,' she said flatly. 'Did you never wonder why Uncle James, an in-law, is Chairman of the Board?'

Anton listened in growing horror as Emily continued.

'Aunt Lisa worked in the offices of Fairfax as a girl. She met and married James, who was employed as the manager at the time and was actually responsible for keeping the firm viable. Grandfather Fairfax had no head for business and spent a fortune on his women. When my father was old enough to join the firm it was James who taught him the ropes and he was twenty-eight when he took over. As a result when my father died it was James he named as Chairman until Tom reaches the age of twenty-eight.'

Emily really was exhausted and, pushing back her chair, she rose to her feet, still holding her napkin. 'So now you know the truth. I am no psychiatrist, but what I was trying to say before was maybe your mother and sister were looking for a father-figure—maybe that's why they behaved the way they did. Who knows?' She shrugged. 'It is amazing how some things affect people. Look at my uncle Clive. You know why he dresses so outrageously and encourages me to?' She smiled. 'Remember the silver lamé?' Then wished she had not said it as she saw Anton grimace in disgust and, nervously twisting the napkin in her hands, she finished. 'Well, Uncle Clive is of the opinion my father and Tom have gone too far the other way. Too conservative, too strait-laced, too frightened of turning out like Grandfather Fairfax, so need shocking once in a while. Maybe he is right. I don't know.'

'Emily.' Anton rose to his feet, and reached out to her, but she took a few hasty steps back.

She didn't want him to touch her; she just wanted the whole sorry mess over with. 'But what I do know is Grandfather Fairfax instead of my father changes nothing. Though I am surprised. You're usually so thorough with your security, your investigators and everything. Why, you never noticed the letter read "*even if I were free which I am not*". That should have given you a clue—when it was written my parents were not even engaged at the time.'

'Emily. I don't know what to say.' Anton reached for her again but she shook off his hand.

'There is nothing to say.' She tilted back her head and looked straight up into his brutally handsome face. 'The truth is out; you were wrong, but right in a way. As usual for you, Anton, you always end up the winner.'

'No, Emily.' He grabbed her by the shoulders. 'I can't tell

you how sorry I am I mixed up your father with your grandfather. I would never have upset you that day on the yacht if I had known. Let me make it up to you somehow. Tell me what you want and it is yours.'

She wanted his love, but he did not have it to give. Sadly she shook her head. 'You don't get it, Anton. Whether it was my father or grandfather does not matter a damn. Nothing has changed—you married me to get back at a Fairfax. And then you wondered why I kept taking the pill. You broke my trust. Can you give that back? I don't think so. Now, if you don't mind I am going to bed and I would like to leave in the morning.' And, turning on her heel, she walked out.

Anton was waiting for her the next morning when she walked downstairs, and simply said, 'The helicopter is here, and my jet is on standby at Lima to take you anywhere you want to go. The apartment in London is yours. I will not be using it again and you have nothing to fear in regard to Fairfax Engineering—I am no longer interested.'

'That is very generous of you,' Emily said, looking up at his expressionless face. Willing him to show the slightest weakness, a gesture he cared. But the black eyes that met hers were cold and hard.

'No doubt we will have to meet again some day, but if you are hoping for a quick divorce, forget it. As far as I am concerned it will not be any time soon. Now, if you will excuse me I have my horses to attend to. I expect you to be gone when I return.'

'Be assured of it,' Emily said coolly. 'As for the divorce, I don't much care when. After this I am not likely to get married again in a hurry. But to ease your mind I don't want a penny of your money. I don't want anything from you, except you keep your promise via a written guarantee you will not interfere in any detrimental way whatsoever with Fairfax Engineering.'

'You will have it,' he snapped, and she watched as he swung on his heel and walked out. She told herself it was for the best, it was what she wanted, and kept telling herself, all the long flight back to London. Then cried herself to sleep in the bed they had shared.

CHAPTER TWELVE

EMILY leant on the rail of the ship, her friend Delia by her side, watching the dinghy taking the divers closer into one of the tiny rocky islands that formed the Las Rocas archipelago off the coast of Venezuela.

'Do you think we will strike lucky this time?' Emily asked.

Delia, older and wiser, grimaced. 'I hope so. It is over a week since we left Caracas, and this is the fourth set of coordinates we have tried, and I don't think we have much more time. I have been checking the weather forecast on the radio and there is a report of a hurricane heading for Florida and on down over the Caribbean islands. It is expected to hit Jamaica, which is not far from us, in three days.'

Emily managed a grin. 'Thanks for the positive report, pal. I think I'll go and check out the computer. It looks like they are ready to dive.' And she went below.

Jake, the head of the expedition, was one of the divers on the dive boat, wanting to explore at close hand the seabed for himself, but his second in command, Marco, was hovering over the bank of computers.

'Anything yet?' she asked.

'No. They have only just reached the site.'

Emily slid into a chair and watched the divers exploring the seabed on the computer screen. Looking for maybe a shape of the prow of a sailing ship or just wood. Or better still the shape of a cannon. After three hundred years anything down there would be buried under sand and encrusted with sea life. Vague silhouettes in the ocean bed could give up the secret of a shipwreck.

It was Emily's job to map the position on the seabed and discern what any find was from the film sent back to the computer by the diver's cameras. She loved her job, and this was the most exciting expedition she had been on so far. Yet somehow, in the five weeks since she had left Peru, she had difficulty getting excited about anything.

She tried not to think of Anton. But he haunted her thoughts day and night. Especially at night as she lay in the bed they had shared. She had yet to tell Helen and Tom that Anton and she had parted. But she knew she was going to have to after this trip. Helen had already started asking pointed questions regarding Anton's whereabouts before Emily left.

Straightening up, Emily fixed her attention on the computer screen. Her marriage was over, done with, and she had to move on. This expedition was the beginning of the rest of her life, she vowed. No more regrets…

Anton steadied the horse between his thighs as the sound of a helicopter disturbed the morning air. Max again…

Two weeks ago Max had found him drunk, and they had had a furious row. Max had told him he was heading for disaster. He had let his wife walk out, a wonderful woman who, if he had any guts, he would be fighting to win back. He was letting his business slide, and ignoring the few friends he had.

Anton had told him to get lost, he knew nothing. But after Max left he had stopped drinking. He had made a few calls consolidating his business interests and delegated the work that could not be avoided to his senior managers. He had no desire to go back to his old life flying around the world. In fact he had no desire for anything with one exception: Emily.

He rode back to the stables and dismounted and handed the reins to the groom. 'Give him a rubdown.' With a pat of the stallion's neck, he walked up to the hacienda.

Max was waiting, a deep frown on his craggy face. 'Why the hell haven't you answered your phone or e-mails?' he demanded. 'I have been trying to get in touch with you since yesterday morning.'

'Hello to you too, Max.'

'At least you look better than the last time I saw you.'

'Yes, well, fresh air and no booze help,' Anton admitted wryly.

'And help is why I am here,' Max said, following Anton into the large hall. 'It's Emily.'

Anton spun around. 'What about her?' he demanded.

'We kept a watch on her, as you said. She stayed in your apartment until ten days ago, when she flew to Caracas.'

'What? Caracas…in Venezuela…?'

'Yes,' Max said with a grimace. 'I know—not the safest place in the world.'

'Was she alone?'

'Yes.' Max nodded.

'Now I need a drink.' Anton strode through into the living room and poured a stiff whisky into a crystal glass and offered one to Max. He shook his head. The thought of a woman like Emily wandering around Venezuela on her own didn't bear thinking about. 'Why, for God's sake?'

'She has joined an expedition led by Jake Hardington and his wife, Delia, friends of Emily's from her university days, apparently. You might have heard of him—the treasure seeker. They hope to find a pirate ship supposedly sunk off the Las

Rocas archipelago by the French navy three hundred years ago. Emily is the marine archaeologist on board.'

Anton stared at his old friend as if he had taken leave of his senses. 'You are telling me that Emily has seriously gone looking for a pirate ship with a bunch of treasure hunters.'

'I know, boss. Strange, but true.'

'Actually, it is not strange.' Anton drained his glass and slammed it down on the counter. 'It is just the damn-fool sort of thing she would do. Why the hell didn't you stop her?'

'You told me to keep a watching brief, nothing more, and get in touch with you if I thought it necessary. I tried to telephone when she left London but you were not answering. I figured, well, it is her line of work, and had my man in Venezuela keep tabs on her. She joined the ship and they set sail on the twentieth, eight days ago. They are at present anchored off a reef. I might add it is not very easy to keep track of them. Treasure seekers are notoriously secretive—they up anchor and move without warning.'

'So why are you here now?'

'Because yesterday there was a hurricane warning. It is heading across the Caribbean and the treasure seekers are not that far from its predicted path. I thought you needed to know. I have hired a high-speed—'

Anton cut him off. 'Five minutes and we leave.'

Emily stood at the rail and watched anxiously as the divers' dinghy ploughed through the heavy waves and finally came alongside. The weather was getting worse by the minute. The wind had risen and the torrential rain had soaked her to the skin. The ship was rolling from side to side making her feel sick. Which was worrying enough in itself, as she had never suffered from seasickness before, but then she had never experienced gale-force winds at sea before.

Everything on board was done at high speed as the threat of drifting onto the reef was imminent. The anchor was lifted, the engines roared and the ship turned to head further out to sea.

Only to see two high-speed Venezuelan navy frigates heading towards them. A loud hailer was utilized demanding they stop, and to everyone's stunned amazement a group of gun-toting sailors boarded them. The ship was seized and ordered back to port and they were all under arrest. Jake tried to ask why but was met by a wall of silence.

Darkness was falling when the ship berthed, not at a commercial port but at a naval base.

Wearing only a cotton tee shirt and shorts, and with her hair and clothes plastered to her body, Emily was beginning to feel afraid as she was led with the others at gunpoint off the vessel.

In the fading light she saw a towering figure approaching. The naval guards parted and her mouth fell open in shock as Anton, ignoring everyone else, strode up to her.

His black eyes were sunken deep and burned like coals of fire in a face that was thinner than she remembered. She had never seen him so angry. Livid...

'That is it, Emily,' he raged, grasping her by the shoulders, his fingers digging into her flesh through the damp cotton. 'What are you trying to do—drive me out of my mind?'

Held close to him, the heat of his body reaching out to her, she shuddered in the old familiar way, though she guessed the heat he generated was more rage than anything else.

'You go off looking for some damn-fool pirate ship in the middle of a hurricane. Well, no more...I have had as much as I am going to take from you. You are coming home with me and that is final. You are not safe to be let out on your own. And I will not be responsible for your death. Hell, even Max can't keep tabs on you.'

'Emily, is this man bothering you?' Jake Hardington asked, moving to face Anton even as recognition of whom he was challenging hit him.

'Bothering her?' Anton snarled. 'I should have talked some sense into her months ago. As for you—how dare you take my wife on your idiotic expedition? I shouldn't have just had you arrested, I should have had you shot.'

'Anton!' Emily exclaimed, finally finding her voice.

'You're his wife?' Jake asked, turning to Emily. 'Anton Diaz's wife?'

'Yes,' she confessed.

Jake looked at Emily and at the man holding her, and whatever he saw made him smile and shake his head. 'You're on your own, Emily.' And stepped back to watch.

'So now you remember you are my wife,' Anton snarled. 'Why the hell could you not have remembered that before you went on this mad adventure? What is it with you? Is it your mission in life to scare me half to death?'

In a state of shock Emily simply let Anton rant on—not that she could have stopped him. He was like a man possessed.

'Why can't you be happy like other women with diamonds and designer clothes and living in the lap of luxury? But no...I had to call out the police force in New York to find you and drop the biggest deal of my life. I had to negotiate with the Venezuelan government to call out the navy to rescue you. Have you the slightest idea what you do to me? You terrify me, Emily, *madre Dios*! Loving you is liable to kill me if you do not bankrupt me first.'

Loving—had Anton said he loved her? And deep down inside a tiny flicker of something very like hope unfurled. Then she stopped thinking as his arms wrapped fiercely around her, moulding her to his hard body, and his mouth crashed down on hers.

The rain poured down on them but Emily was oblivious to everything but Anton. His mouth ravaged hers with a passion that bordered on violence and she clung to him, her hands linking behind his neck, and returned his kiss with a hunger, a desperate need she could not deny.

She moved restlessly against him, her wet clothing and his accentuating the hard pressure of his arousal against her belly.

'Hell, Emily, you could have died.' He groaned and buried his head in her throat, sucking on the pulse that beat madly there, his hands feverishly roaming up and down her body. 'Are you sure you are all right?' He groaned again and lifted his head, his hair plastered like a black skullcap to his scalp, and to Emily he had never looked better.

'Did you say you loved me?' was the only question in her mind.

'Love you...' He paused, and glanced away to the people surrounding them. His dark eyes returned to her upraised face, and, in a curiously reverent gesture, he pressed a kiss to her brow, each soft cheek. 'Yes, I love you, Emily Diaz.' And his lips curved in a wry smile. 'Why else would I be standing here making a complete and utter fool of myself in front of all these people?'

Emily had spent too long mistrusting him and thinking he was not capable of loving anyone to immediately believe him. Her blue eyes, wide and wary, searched his haggard features, looking for some sign that would convince her.

'Damn it, Emily,' Jake Hardington cut in. 'The man loves you, tell him you love him, and let us get out of here. In case you have not noticed, the rest of us are still standing here with guns pointed at us and Diaz is the only one who can set us free.'

Startled, Emily looked at Jake and back at Anton. 'Is that right?'

'Right that I love you, and right I can set them free. The other is up to you.' And she saw a hint of vulnerability in his eyes and her own softened as the hope inside her burst into flame.

They had a lot to sort out, she knew, but she had to take the risk and tell him she loved him if they were to have a future together. But she never got the chance to speak.

'But either way I am not setting you free,' Anton added, his arms tightening around her.

Emily burst out laughing. That was *so* Anton—vulnerable for seconds but quickly as arrogant and indomitable as ever. 'Oh, Anton, I do love you.' And, reaching up, she kissed him as a round of applause broke out.

'At last, Emily, and now you have got your husband in a good mood, get him to sponsor my next expedition,' Jake Hardington called out. 'Because he wrecked this one.'

Anton looked at Jake. 'Hardington, you are pushing your luck.' But he smiled, taking the sting out of his words, and, sweeping Emily up in his arms with a few instructions to the officer in charge, he carried her away.

The hotel was luxurious and Anton paced the sitting room of the two-bedroomed suite listening to the sound of the bath running. Emily was in there, and he ached to join her. But, instead, on arriving he had told her to go ahead and have a bath and he would order dinner from room service. He had done it though he had never felt less like eating in his life. He had quickly showered in the *en suite* of the other bedroom and was now wearing a white towelling robe courtesy of the hotel, pacing the floor like an idiot.

For some bizarre reason he was ridiculously nervous. This love thing was a whole lot harder than he had ever imagined— not that he ever had imagined, he admitted self-derisively. With damp palms, a pounding heart and a churning stomach, he had a whole new respect for love.

Emily had said she loved him, but it had been with an audience urging her on. She had said she loved him on their wedding night, but the next day, when he had made the catastrophic mistake about her father, she had changed her mind. How could he know she was certain she loved him now?

It was his own fault and he had spent what seemed like ages running over and over in his head what he would say to her. How he would apologize to her for his past mistakes. Straightening his shoulders, he walked into the bedroom. He had it all planned in his head. All he needed was Emily.

Emily slipped on the hotel's towelling robe and, barefoot, exited the bathroom happier than she had ever been. Anton was standing in the middle of the room, a serious expression on his handsome face. 'Anton,' she said rather shyly, 'did you order dinner?'

His dark head lifted. 'Yes.' And in two lithe strides he was beside her. '*Dio*! Emily, how can you ever forgive me?' Anton groaned. 'When I think what I have said and done since we met I cringe.' And placing an arm around her, he pulled her close. 'That first day on the boat you called me dumb and I was...' He curved a strong hand around the nape of her neck and tilted her head up to his. 'My only excuse is I didn't know if I was on my head or my heels.'

'It does not matter now, Anton,' Emily said softly. 'The past is behind us. People say the first six months of marriage are the worst, so we have two more to go,' she tried to joke.

'I could not stand another two minutes, never mind months, at odds with you.' He lifted her and laid her gently on the bed and stretched his long length out next to her. 'I need to tell you this, Emily. To confess, if you like,' he said, his dark eyes serious as, propped on one arm, he looked down at her.

'Couldn't it wait?' She smiled impishly up at him. His robe had fallen open and she rested her hand lightly on his broad chest.

'No.' He caught her hand in his and linked their fingers. His dark gaze lingered on the gold band on her finger for a moment. 'I have done a lot of soul-searching over the last few weeks, and I want you to hear me out and make you understand why I behaved as I did.'

'Do I have to? I can think of better things to do.' She grinned.

'Yes,' Anton said sternly, if a little regretfully. 'After my mother died, naturally I was upset, and finding out about Suki only made me worse. I am not good with emotions and my grief turned to anger and I vented my fury on the Fairfax family. But if you believe nothing else, believe this—from the minute I saw you I fell in love with you. I know that now, but at the time I would not admit it even to myself.'

He paused for a moment, looking deep into her eyes, willing her to believe in him, and then continued at breakneck speed. 'I did not believe in love because I had seen what it did to my mother and sister. But with hindsight, much as I loved them they were basically weak, not like my grandmother. The day I proposed to you I was mad with jealousy because I thought you had dressed so strikingly for another man. The day you walked down the aisle in church I knew the image of you would be etched on my brain for ever. Watching you sleep on the jet, I decided I was not going to tell you about your father.

'Our wedding night was the most amazing night of my life. You were everything and more than I could ever have imagined, your husky words of love much more than I deserved, which in my arrogance I took as my due.' He gave her a rueful grin. 'But you know what happened the next day—I lost my temper when you mentioned your parents and told you anyway about your father. But the truth was I was feeling as guilty as hell. I couldn't believe I had been dumb enough to think for a minute my yearly trip to Monte Carlo was suitable as a honeymoon. At one point I considered just telling the captain to set sail and leave everyone behind, but it was too late.

'Then the whole weekend went from bad to worse. I behaved like an arrogant swine. You nearly gave me a heart attack diving off the yacht and that damn Harding woman filled your head with lies about me.'

'It really does not matter,' Emily said, lifting a hand to stroke his lean cheek. Though his revelations filled her heart to overflowing with love.

'Yes, it does to me. When you told me to find another woman for the night, it gutted me. I spent hours pacing the deck before returning to bed, and realizing it wasn't your fault. You were angry and had every right to be.

'Then in Greece in my conceit I thought everything was wonderful. It wasn't until we were due to leave when I saw you walking down the stairs in the suit you had worn after our wedding that I recognized what was missing. You had looked at me with such joy, such love, when you walked towards me when we were about to leave Deveral Hall that day, but not any more. And I saw the difference. We made love but you never said the word. You never said much at all. I told myself it didn't matter. But on the spur of the moment I crazily decided to take you to New York instead of London. I could not leave you without trying to change things, though I had no idea how.'

'You were actually going to take me to London and instead you kidnapped me.' Emily chuckled. 'All because of a blue suit.'

'Yes. But then you got lost and as I stormed out of a meeting without a second thought I knew I was in serious trouble, but I was still in denial about my true feelings.'

'You were angry, and did seem a little upset when we got back to the apartment. I actually wondered if you cared.'

'Cared.' He grimaced. 'Oh, I cared. But the real clincher, the moment it hit me right between the eyes, was in the limousine on the way back from the exhibition of Peruvian art, when you asked me why had I not married Lucita to get back at her father. I realized it had never occurred to me, and it wouldn't have done in a million years, and yet the two cases were in a way similar. Then I had to ask myself why you?'

'It was a completely outlandish idea. I had been a bachelor for thirty-seven years and no woman had even tempted me to get married before. So why was I so determined to marry you? I am not proud of the fact, but I could have ruined your family business, but I think it was grief that fuelled my vengeance more than anything else. I needed someone to blame. But by the time I met Tom and James I was already losing enthusiasm for the project, because there was nothing to dislike about them. Quite the reverse—I had a grudging respect for them, and then I met you, Emily…

'To be totally frank, I took one look at you and could not stop myself flirting with you rather crudely.' He grimaced again. 'Then I saw you dancing with Max, and that was it.'

Anton dropped her hand and lifted a finger to her lips and gently outlined the contours of her mouth. 'All I could think of was your lithesome body under mine. You were the most sensuous woman I had ever seen. But at the time I thought anyone who danced like you must have had a few lovers and I was going to be one of them.'

'What exactly did you intend to do?' Emily asked. 'Make me your mistress?'

'No. I decided before the music ended, I was going to marry you. Your effect on me was that instant. In my arrogance I decided you would make a wonderful wife and mother.' His expression darkened. 'It was you who thought I wanted a mistress, as I found out just before we parted.' His dark eyes held hers, intent and oddly resigned. 'I know I had no right, but I was outraged to discover you were taking the pill without telling me. I felt used like some stud to perform in bed and nothing more. Not good enough to be the father of your children.'

'Oh, Anton.' Emily looped her arms around his neck and looked deep into his eyes. 'I never thought that for a second. I loved you even when I didn't want to. But you told me you did not believe in love, civil and sex you said, and I did not think our marriage could possibly last. I did not think you could stay faithful; I was green with jealousy thinking about all your other women, and knowing you did not love me made it worse.'

'I am sorry, Emily, so sorry.' He groaned. 'I never intended to hurt you. I love you, and if you don't want children that is okay by me, but I cannot let you go. I love you so much it hurts,' he declared, and she was stunned by the flicker of pain in the dark depth of his eyes that he could not hide.

Emily was shocked that he really thought she did not want his baby. Shocked that such a strong, wonderful man, a man she had thought without emotion, could be so emotionally vulnerable. She was suddenly conscious of the heavy pounding of her heart and his, the lengthening silence and his stillness... He was afraid... Surely not.

She slipped her hands up and around his neck, and smiled brilliantly up at him. 'How about you stop talking and show me some of this love you talk about?'

'You mean that—you really do love me?' Anton asked, his dark eyes gleaming down into hers, and she urged him closer.

'Yes,' she breathed. 'But as for a baby...' She felt him

stiffen. 'I think you might be too late—I am already almost four weeks late.'

Anton's brutally handsome features clenched in a frown. 'What…? How…? When…?' He loved Emily, but she had an amazing ability to confuse his normally needle-sharp brain without even trying.

'The how you know.' She laughed up at him. 'The when and where are the last time we were in London. I had forgotten to take my pills for the two days I stayed at Helen's—when you found me I was trying to catch up…'

'Do you mind?' he asked, tension in every line of his great body.

'No—if I am right, I am delighted. I would love to have your baby, but right now I would love to have you,' she said boldly, her sparkling blue eyes lit with amusement and something more fixed on his, one long leg wrapping over his as she turned into him.

Anton's arms wrapped around her convulsively as the import of her words sank in. He almost yelled what the hell was she doing on the damn-fool expedition then? But stopped in time. She was Emily. Beautiful, wonderful, wilful, but his Emily and he would not have her any other way.

'Thank the Lord.' He groaned, his heart in his eyes as he bent his head and kissed her with all the tender passion and love in his soul.

Dinner was delivered; the waiter called out, and was met with a particularly appropriate Spanish expletive. He smiled. He was a man and he had been in service long enough to recognize it was a different appetite on the occupant's mind, and left the trolley in the sitting room and tiptoed out.

HARLEQUIN *Presents*

Harlequin Presents brings you
a brand-new duet by star author

Sharon Kendrick

THE GREEK BILLIONAIRES' BRIDES

Possessed by two Greek billionaire brothers

Alexandros Pavlidis always ended his affairs before
boredom struck. After a passionate relationship with
Rebecca Gibbs, he never expected to see her again.
Until she arrived at his office—pregnant, with twins!

Don't miss

THE GREEK TYCOON'S CONVENIENT WIFE,

on sale July 2008

THE BOSS'S MISTRESS

Out of the office…and into his bed

These ruthless, powerful men are used
to having their own way in the office—
and with their mistresses they're also
boss in the bedroom!

**Don't miss any of our fantastic stories
in the July 2008 collection:**

Inside ROMANCE

Stay up-to-date on all your romance reading news!

Inside Romance is a FREE quarterly newsletter highlighting our upcoming series releases and promotions.

Visit
www.eHarlequin.com/InsideRomance
to sign up to receive our complimentary newsletter today!

IRNI107

REQUEST YOUR FREE BOOKS!

HARLEQUIN *Presents*®

2 FREE NOVELS PLUS 2 FREE GIFTS!

PASSION GUARANTEED SEDUCTION

YES! Please send me 2 FREE Harlequin Presents® novels and my 2 FREE gifts (gifts are worth about $10). After receiving them, if I don't wish to receive any more books, I can return the shipping statement marked "cancel". If I don't cancel, I will receive 6 brand-new novels every month and be billed just $4.05 per book in the U.S. or $4.74 per book in Canada, plus 25¢ shipping and handling per book and applicable taxes, if any*. That's a savings of close to 15% off the cover price! I understand that accepting the 2 free books and gifts places me under no obligation to buy anything. I can always return a shipment and cancel at any time. Even if I never buy another book, the two free books and gifts are mine to keep forever.

106 HDN ERRW 306 HDN ERRL

Name _____ (PLEASE PRINT)

Address _____ Apt. #

City _____ State/Prov. _____ Zip/Postal Code

Signature (if under 18, a parent or guardian must sign)

Mail to the Harlequin Reader Service:

IN U.S.A.: P.O. Box 1867, Buffalo, NY 14240-1867
IN CANADA: P.O. Box 609, Fort Erie, Ontario L2A 5X3

Not valid to current subscribers of Harlequin Presents books.

Want to try two free books from another line?
Call 1-800-873-8635 or visit www.morefreebooks.com.

* Terms and prices subject to change without notice. N.Y. residents add applicable sales tax. Canadian residents will be charged applicable provincial taxes and GST. This offer is limited to one order per household. All orders subject to approval. Credit or debit balances in a customer's account(s) may be offset by any other outstanding balance owed by or to the customer. Please allow 4 to 6 weeks for delivery. Offer available while quantities last.

Your Privacy: Harlequin Books is committed to protecting your privacy. Our Privacy Policy is available online at www.eHarlequin.com or upon request from the Reader Service. From time to time we make our lists of customers available to reputable third parties who may have a product or service of interest to you. If you would prefer we not share your name and address, please check here. ☐

HP08